ZHŪ

ZHŪ

式

J. R. BRIENZA

MILL CITY PRESS

Mill City Press, Inc.
2301 Lucien Way #415
Maitland, FL 32751
407.339.4217
www.millcitypress.net

Printed in the United States of America

ISBN-13: 978-1-54566-426-1

"I am fond of pigs.
Dogs look up to us.
Cats look down on us.
Pigs treat us as equals."
Winston Churchill

Contents

Chapter 1

A Promise Is A Promise

City streets clamored with rush hour activity. The workaday world raced from offices and factories to be at their loved ones side, as the twilight grew. Street lights flickered to life along the hospital courtyard.

For Maxwell Sutherland, there would be no bustle. That evening, he already sat at his loved one's side. His wife's death bed.

Waves of pain washed over her pasty, wrinkled face. She was a beauty, __once. Long before time, and the ravages of her illness took their toll. She grimaced as another tremor punished her body, trembling with weakness.

"Oooh!" she cried out, while lacing her fingers over her lower abdomen, an attempt to support the child that kicked in her belly.

Maxwell wasted no time. He soothed her tummy with one hand, while wiping sweat from her brow with the other. The unborn elbowed the palm of his hand for his effort.

"I wish."

"Maxwell, please." She huffed to catch her breath. "Don't."

"I know, but maybe if you weren't pregnant, we could have concentrated on getting you well. We could have bought you more time."

"She has given me that time. Don't you see? I have always wanted to be a mother. Bringing her into the world is the only thing that has kept me here this l-long. Oooh! OOOW!"

Maxwell thought about the pre-natal screenings, and how the baby carried the same genetic mutation as his wife. His throat ached with a sadness that settled into his chest, as he watched her belly move. One life eager to come in, and with each bout of agony, another life, dying to get out. As wealthy and powerful as he was, there was nothing he could do about any of it.

"OOOH! OOOW!"

The electronic gauges monitoring her blared an urgent warning. The room filled with hospital staff, and even more equipment.

Maxwell held his wife in his arms, and kissed her cheek. She whispered in his ear. Before he could reply, they pulled him away, kicking and screaming to the safe distance of the hallway.

"I promise!" He screamed as they shut the door behind him.

He watched the frenzied work, nose and hands pressed to the glass, until a nurse pulled the drapery closed in front of his face. When the room became quiet, he realized that the kiss would be his last. Gravity slid him down the wall, landing him at a seat on the floor with legs outstretched. Doctors and nurses filed out, one by one. They offered sympathy with their medical speak, but all that Maxwell Sutherland could hear was his wife pleading in his ear.

"Don't let our baby die!"

Chapter 2

Little Girl Lost

"What now?" asked Maxwell Sutherland. He stroked his daughter Abby's cheek with his index finger. "There must be another option. I swore to do everything possible for her." He cupped her fragile face in his hands. "That's a promise I intend to keep."

The child lay, unconscious in the hospital bed that had become her prison. A pretty prison it was, too. A yellow and blue floral chintz canopy hung in a semicircle above the institutional set of mattresses and machinery. Matching drapery clung to the pair of French doors that overlooked the garden. A garden that Abby was never likely to see.

"She is on the transplant list, but it is long, and there are so many ahead of her," Dr. Liu commiserated, "but, perhaps there is *-something.*"

"I'm listening." Sutherland's eyes never looked up from his eight year old daughter.

"Well," continued Liu, "I have a colleague, former roommate, actually. He's doing some remarkable work, ground breaking stuff. The man is a true visionary. He's about to set the transplant world on its ear. Of course, his work is thought to be quite controversial, if not illegal, here in the U.S., but he may offer a solution. He is in China, and no doubt he is quite expensive, and then there are legal implications that could prove to be tricky_"

"For crying out loud, Liu, what are you blathering on about? Get to the point."

Dr. Liu stood firmly, with his hands to his sides. "Have you ever heard of the Chimera Collaborative?"

Maxwell Sutherland puzzled for a moment, as the last of the daylight gave the chintz drapery a soft orange glow.

"Uh, I can't say that I have. Isn't a chimera some grotesque creature out of mythology? Something with parts of different kinds of animals like a centaur that is half horse, half human, or the winged monkeys in the Wizard of Oz?"

"Yes, you are correct, but what I speak of, is the Chimera Collaborative, a scientific breakthrough headed up by Dr. Shen Duan. His team has pioneered the technique of growing human organs in pig embryos."

The rhythmic hiss of Abby's respirator, sighed in disbelief. Maxwell Sutherland wasn't convinced either.

"So, we are going to give my daughter pig kidneys, are we?"

Dr. Liu smiled tentatively. "No, not *exactly*."

Chapter 3

Strike a Bargain

"It's all there. Seventy two point five million in unmarked Swiss francs. Feel free to count it."

The armored car staffer drove a Skid Steer Loader into Dr. Duan's sizeable laboratory. Carefully, he stacked the last five pallets into the center of the room. Each was over three feet high, and wrapped tightly in plastic shrink wrap.

"Count it?" asked Dr, Duan. "But of course!" He nodded, and two men in white lab coats proceeded to un-wrap the pallets and fire up the electric counting machines. "Have you my other precious cargo?" he asked.

Dr. Liu handed a small white cooler to Dr. Duan. "Human donor cells as per your instructions."

"Hao!" shouted one of the men counting the cash.

"Good, very good," remarked Dr. Duan. "It seems that your honorable American tycoon can count accurately. I am pleased."

"I'd like to confirm a few contractual details, specifically lead time. We have a very sick child to attend to." Dr. Liu began to take notes into his hand held device.

Dr. Duan nodded, but remained expressionless. "As per our agreement, I will use a wild pig embryo, to ensure a longer life span of the Chimera. We may get as many as eighteen years out of it, compared to an average of eight years for a domesticated pig. I think this is necessary given the severity of Mr. Sutherland's daughter's illness, and the likelihood of the need for multiple harvests. Given a gestation period of one hundred fourteen days, plus a simple battery of tests to ensure the Chimera's viability, and a genetic match. I can deliver in six months from today."

"And if the child dies while waiting for delivery?"

"Oh, a pity, to be sure, but let us hope for the best. I am engineering a custom product, tailored to the specific needs of that child. The deposit is, as I have indicated in our contract, *non-refundable.*"

"I'll be seeing you in six months, then," said Dr. Liu. Doctors Liu and Duan shook hands.

"Yes, I'll be seeing you both," answered Duan.

"Us both?"

"Yes, both you, *and* the balance of Seventy two point five million Swiss Francs."

Chapter 4

Money to Burn

Six months passed quickly for all except Abby Sutherland, the girl whose strange, cancer-like illness has now spread to both of her kidneys, and her father, who watched the child suffer daily in pain.

A full time staff of doctors and nurses tended to her, administering chemotherapy treatments, the best they could do with something so rare. All hoped they could keep the cells from spreading to other vital organs, but there was never a guarantee, especially since they weren't entirely sure of what they were dealing with.

Maxwell Sutherland checked the shimmering blue face of his Rolex Milgauss.

"Three P.M." he thought. "Dr. Liu should be arriving in China, right about now."

The Sutherland Industries jet landed without delay or incident at Beijing Capital International Airport. Once again, the mall Skid Steer unloaded the palettes of unmarked bills, placing them carefully into the armored car that would deliver the king's ransom to the labs of Dr. Duan.

This particular part of his task amused Liu. He wondered at the skill and precision of the bribes that Maxwell Sutherland paid to ensure that millions of dollars could travel from the U.S. to China without taxes, tariffs, or the slightest bit of scrutiny.

"Hao!" shouted one of the men in white lab coats from the office.

"Aah, your employer is an honorable man. The funds are accounted for. Follow me," said Dr. Duan.

A series of brightly lit corridors gave way to a single hospital room. The fluorescent light in the room's center sputtered and flickered an irksome Morris Code.

"Perhaps you'd like to inspect the merchandise? A physical examination is in order, to say the least. I'm very proud of our finished product. I'm certain you and your good Mr. Sutherland will be most pleased."

Dr. Duan walked to the gurney, and pulled back the top sheet. “I have named him Zhū.”

“My God, Duan! What have you done?”

Chapter 5

Speedy Delivery

"So nice to have you back on American soil, Dr. Liu." Sutherland swiveled his oxblood leather desk chair in Liu's direction. He took a puff from his pipe. The tobacco was sweet and light. The smoke hung like thin cirrus clouds of a summer day. "So, how did it go? I hope I got my money's worth. Good thing you're back. In the nick of time, I'd say. Abby still isn't responding to the chemo. We have to move quickly. How fast can you assemble your team, and ready the Chimera?"

"Yes, Mr. Sutherland, it went well, quite well, indeed. And the Chimera is very healthy, Sir, but I."

"But what? Spit it out, already!"

"I, uh, I think you should come have a look at the Chimera for yourself, Sir."

"But you said it is healthy, you're the expert here. If this thing isn't what I paid for, I'd hope you'd have enough sense to withhold the balance of the Francs until that Dr. Duan character made the necessary corrections."

"No Sir, it isn't that. I assure you, the Chimera is a perfectly healthy organism, and a genetic match for Abby."

"So what's the problem?"

"Come look for yourself," suggested Dr. Liu, as they walked to the new wing.

While waiting for the delivery from Dr. Duan, an onsite state of the art surgical suite was built on the grounds of Sutherland Knoll. The labyrinth of labs and treatment rooms adjoined Abby's bedroom. It contained the best medical equipment money could buy, courtesy of Maxwell Sutherland's very deep pockets.

Dr. Liu admired the facilities. He pulled a stainless steel stool toward Maxwell and gestured toward it. "Perhaps you had better sit down," he patted the cold hard seat.

"I'm fine. Let's have a look at the thing, I haven't got all day."

Dr. Liu steeled himself for his task. He donned a pair of latex gloves in a quick and efficient snap, but hesitated to pull the sheet away. Beads of sweat formed on his brow, and upper lip. His stomach fluttered while his heart pounded in his ears. Liu was less than eager to lay eyes on the Chimera once more.

"Get on with it!"

Deciding that the shock of seeing the entire Chimera might be too much for Mr. Sutherland, as it was for him. Dr. Liu thought it would be best to expose just a small section of science's most advanced development, and turned back the top eighteen inches of the sheet.

"Um," choke, "well, I say, uh…"

Maxwell Sutherland made a bee line for the stainless steel stool, concluding that having a seat might be a good idea, after all.

"Not what you expected, Mr. Sutherland?"

"Well, uh, I'm not certain what I expected, but uh, this is it, eh?"

Dr. Liu pulled the sheet down a bit more.

"No, no!" Maxwell Sutherland used the heels of his Italian loafers to slide the stool away at an angle. "That won't be necessary. I have seen quite enough, thank you. Meet me back in my office in one hour."

Maxwell stood, and turned away from Dr. Liu. He smoothed his furrowed brow with is left hand. The glint of his gold wedding ring was a stern reminder of his daughter Abby, the dying little girl asleep in the next room. No matter how disturbing the Chimera, it was a development that would save Abby's life. This technology wasn't available when his wife was ill, affording her fewer options at survival. He took hold of the silver door lever that would set him free from all he had seen. It would enable him to escape his concerns, distance him from his own conflict and guilt that Abby's mother was not alive to see their child grow up.

"What would you like me to do? with the Chimera, I mean."

Maxwell's decision had been made. He knew exactly what he had to do with the Chimera. "Why, schedule the surgery, of course!"

Chapter 6

Staffing Issues

Two groups of nurses and surgeons assembled themselves around the sink, scrubbing up for the kidney harvest. Team one would be dedicated to the organ's removal, closing up, and stabilizing the Chimera. Team two would transplant the harvest to the gravely ill Abby Sutherland. A delicate and complex procedure awaited the group, and the gravity of their undertaking weighed heavily on them all.

The anesthesia nurse prepared the Chimera, but stopped in her tracks. Her hands trembled.

"I - I don't think I can be part of this," her voice cracked.

"Come on, Nurse Morton. You have been briefed, as we all have. You know the Sutherland girl's case as well as anyone. What issues do you have that could not have been addressed well before we begin surgery?"

"What issues?" asked the nurse. "Just look at it! Let's call that issue number one."

Both teams muttered and whispered among themselves.

Dr. Liu feared that he was about to lose them. All of them. "Nurse Morton, let's go. We're going to talk about this out in the hall. Get Eric from team two. He'll sub for her. Anyone else suddenly conflicted with this transplant? Anyone?"

The others were suddenly quiet. None raised their hand or made any indication that they weren't willing or able to proceed. Most kept busy by scrubbing up.

Liu removed his mask, coat and gloves in the hall. "I don't understand. You're a pro. The best pediatric anesthesia nurse bar none. Why start a revolt just as we're about to save that little girl's life?"

"For starters. I can't agree to a regional anesthesia on the Chimera. We're discussing kidney removal here!" Her voice cracked again. "Would you remove Abby Sutherland's diseased organs under regional anesthetic?"

"No, but Abby Sutherland is a human child, the pain would be unbearable. It isn't the same thing. The Chimera is *not* human."

"Isn't human?" she challenged. "The Chimera? It was formed with human stem cells, and well, you have eyes. Just look at it!"

"There is no need to raise your voice, Nurse." Dr. Liu said with ice in his words. "I can see that your mind is made up." He pressed a button on the hallway wall. A pair of security guards appeared. "You are fired. Collect your belongings in the women's locker. Security will see you to your car. I trust Legal won't have to contact you for any breech related to the non-disclosure agreement that you signed."

As cold as Dr. Liu was on the outside, his heart warmed to the Chimera lying on a table in the surgical suite, about to have a kidney removed. Nurse Morton was right. She merely voiced a portion of what concerns he himself had. The pain inflicted on the Chimera was just one worry. The other was the question of consent. Little Abby Sutherland could not make decisions regarding her health, but her father was her advocate, her voice, her protector. Who did the Chimera have?

Dr. Liu went back to scrubbing. He was committed to this case. He himself was responsible for the Chimera being there, and he was also dedicated to saving Abby from the ravages of her malady. Between the two positions was a tight spot, indeed. He concluded that he would save Abby Sutherland's life, *and* he would protect the helpless organism that was unable to speak for itself.

"Anesthesia, change of plans. Nurse Morton will *not* be joining us. Nurse Eric, you've just earned double time. I've also decided that we will *not* administer a regional. The Chimera will have general anesthesia. Let's get to work."

Chapter 7
Team Players

Maxwell Sutherland lifted his pipe from its crystal resting place, and filled it with aromatic tobacco while Dr. Liu updated him on the procedures, and Abby's prognosis.

"Removing the Chimera's kidney was the most challenging part of the procedures. Ultra sound, and our surgical cameras allowed pinpoint accuracy for identifying location, etcetera, but the Chimera's renal artery and renal vein, were both more difficult to detach, and the connecting tissue far more sinewy than we'd expect from our experience with human children."

Maxwell stirred in his chair. "I know you have assembled the finest teams possible."

"Indeed, I have, and they have excelled. They have given their best for you, and for Abby."

Maxwell puffed on his pipe. He exhaled, a sleepy dragon, emitting chocolate cherry scorched breath. "I'm told you have lost a very fine member of team one. Is that true?"

Dr. Liu loosened the draw string on his scrubs, and fidgeted in the oxblood barrel chair that kept him from collapsing from exhaustion, on to the chestnut parquet floors of Maxwell Sutherland's office.

"Yes, that is true. A pediatric anesthesiology nurse. Team one, as you say."

"I hear she nearly caused both teams to cut and run. You must be more careful in screening candidates. If you need more clerical, or a better psychology team to analyze doctor and nurse profiles, whatever, tell me what you need, and it's yours. I won't have another team member putting Abby at risk."

"Thank you. A more in depth psychological evaluation for candidates might just be what we need. Please rest assured that the situation was not as dire as you were led to believe. She and I discussed her concerns in the hallway, *privately*."

"Concerns?" Maxwell removed the pipe from his mouth.

Dr. Liu breathed a lung full of aromatic second-hand smoke. "She took sudden ethical issues with the kidney harvest. Issues that she made no indication of during the briefing, but when faced with the visual inventory of the Chimera, she- *she froze*."

Maxwell tapped his pipe with his index finger, then dumped the spent remains of the tobacco into a marble bowl. "So you fired her."

"Yes. She was a liability, a risk, not just to the Chimera, but to Abby. She had to go."

"When can I look in on Abby?"

A loud crash echoed down the long corridor from the surgical suite to Maxwell Sutherland's home office.

"Squeaaaaaal squeal, squeaaaaal!"

Maxwell dropped his favorite pipe on the desk top. His eyebrows wrinkled in question. For a moment he wondered if he might be hearing things.

"Squeaaaaal, squeal, squeaaaaal!"

"There it is again!" exclaimed Maxwell.

Dr. Liu bolted from his comfy leather chair to the door, and excused himself in a blur of black hair and blue scrubs.

"What is happening?"

Dr. Liu's voice trailed behind him as he ran down the corridor.

"The Chimera!"

Chapter 8

Liquid Gold

Dr. Liu burst through the doors of the surgical suite.

"Squeaaaaal squeal squeaaal!" The Chimera's booming cries echoed throughout the room, the sound bouncing off of the hard surfaces. "Squeaaaal squeal squeaaaal!"

"The restraints are holding, but it is likely to cause itself harm. Look at the bruising that's already started," said Nurse Vicki.

"Squeaaaal squeal squeaaaal!"

"Let's start it with 2.5 milligrams morphine sulphate. That should address the discomfort. I want the Chimera closely monitored for signs of reaction," said Dr. Liu. *Amazing that it has come out of the anesthesia so quickly.* He thought.

Liu scrolled through the notes the attending left on the computer. *Vitals all look good. Remarkably good, and the Chimera has already urinated – an excellent sign after just losing a kidney.* The nurse administered the morphine through a port installed in the Chimera prior to the harvest.

"Squeaaaal! Squeal! Squeaaal!" The Chimera still thrashed on the gurney, while the nurse adjusted the drip.

"DADDY!" Abby cried out in pain. Another nurse entered, and beckoned Dr. Liu to join her at the girl's side.

"She started to come out from under sedation about the same time as the Chimera. I've started her drip. Her chart is complete, and ready for your review," said the nurse.

Once again, Dr. Liu was astonished. The girl had two diseased kidneys removed, and a new one installed, but her vitals were strong, and she was awake in record time.

Maxwell Sutherland entered in a full mask, gloves, and gown. "I heard Abby cry out for me. I want to see her. Is she okay? Why is she awake so soon?" The worry lines around his eyes deepened with concern. He rushed to her.

“Daddy!” she cried, “It hurts! It hurts, Daddy.” Tears ran down her face.

“The nice nurse has just given you something for the pain, honey.” A nurse emptied a syringe into her line, and nodded confirmation. “I promise you’ll be feeling better very soon.” He wiped Abby’s eyes, and kissed her forehead through his mask.

“Daddy”- Abby’s soft voice trailed off, and in moments, she was sound asleep.

“Tell me some good news, DR,” huffed Maxwell.

“You’ll have a full report in the morning. Please, Sir, get some sleep, and rest assured that it is *very* good news.” Dr. Liu lifted the side of the sheet that hung down from Abby’s bed, to expose a drainage bag from Abby’s catheter. The bag had an inch of yellow liquid as its contents.

“Urine?” asked Maxwell.

“Yes, Sir!” replied an enthusiastic Liu.

“It’s working? The kidney is working?”

Dr. Liu smiled, and breathed deeply.

“Like a charm.”

Chapter 9

General Maintenance

Daily meetings regarding Abby's post-transplant progress had become the norm. In a few short weeks, Abby was showing no signs of rejection, and was moving to solid food. She was bright eyed, pink cheeked, and as responsive as a normal, healthy child.

"I'm encouraged by all of it," said Maxwell.

"As am I, Mr. Sutherland. Abby is doing as well as any of the team dared hope. We do, however, have to determine the Chimera's status, moving forward," answered Dr. Liu.

"What about it? I thought you were just keeping the thing sedated?" Maxwell opened a fresh bag of tobacco.

"True. We are. A benzodiazepine drip, with a daily sedation holiday has been the norm, but this is not safe in the days and perhaps years ahead. Especially on an organism so young. There are too many risks in continuing this indefinitely."

Maxwell lit his pipe with a table top lighter shaped like a miniature suit of armor. He puffed as he formulated his next question. "What are the risks?" he asked.

"Bradycardia hypotention, Q.T. prolongation, respiratory depression, rebound hypertension, and of course, renal failure, remember, the Chimera is using one kidney."

"In English?" Maxwell bristled.

"Simply stated, the health of the Chimera will be greatly compromised under constant sedation. In order to help Abby as best as we can, it is crucial that the Chimera is as healthy as possible for future harvests. Plus, I think it is just the right thing to do for him, to provide him with some quality of life."

Maxwell stood at his desk. He puffed some more. "I'd agree that it is in Abby's best interest to keep the thing heathy, Dr. Liu, but let's not forget that the Chimera is nothing more than an expensive medical device. That's it, a device, one to be properly maintained to be sure, the thing did cost me a fortune, after all. By all means, maintain it as you see fit, but spare me the bleeding heart compassionate, quality of life nonsense."

Dr. Liu squirmed in his seat. Mentally, he made his plan for moving Abby to another room, perhaps in the north wing, overlooking the partierres. *Housekeeping would have to be notified, and of course the medical staff,* Liu thought.

"Quality of life?" Maxwell fumed under his breath. "Ridiculous." He paused for a moment, then squinted at Dr.Liu. "Did you say, he?"

"The Chimera is most definitely a *he.* That "very expensive medical device" has the male genitalia of a pre-pubescent human."

Chapter 10

Ham it up

A team of nurses, orderlies, and housekeeping made the move of Abby Sutherland to a room in the north wing. The room was larger than her previous one, adjacent to the surgical suite. The décor also much more adult than the pale yellow and baby blue chintz from her former space. The walls wore a terra cotta paint, the color of the Arizona desert. The rug on the floor covered most of the walnut parquet. It was a riotous cluster of apricot roses with chartreuse foliage on a chocolate field. The drapery was made of an apricot damask with tassel fringe in varying shades of green, terra cotta and brown. The effect pulled the colors of the garden's boxwood partierres and roses into the room, and in turn, the room, out into the garden.

The quilted bedspread was turned down, as an orderly lifted Abby from her wheel chair to the bed.

"But I'm not sleepy! I don't want to go to bed! I'm bored!" protested Abby.

"Dr. Liu's orders, I'm afraid," consoled Nurse Vicki while Abby pouted. "Here are your dolls. Lunch should be here soon. What do you say to video games after you've eaten? I think that might cure a case of the blahs."

An orderly set a tray on a wheeled cart in front of Abby.

"See, I told you lunch would be here in no time." The nurse took the steel covers off of the plates, exposing Abby's meal.

The girl turned up her nose as she peeled back the top layer of bread to reveal a slice of cheese, and cold slivers of ham. She grimaced, and pushed the plate away.

"Oh no you don't young lady. The deal was video games *after* you eat. Got it?"

"Yes, but."

"But what? Aren't you hungry?"

"I'm hungry." Abby touched her tummy.

"Okay, then eat! The sooner you finish, the sooner I can whip you at a game of Bonbon Bash."

"But I, I don't want it."

The nurse examined the tray, and pushed the sandwich closer to Abby. Looks like your favorite lunch to me. Why don't you want it? You love ham and cheese sandwiches.

"I do?" questioned Abby. She turned her head away and squinted, as to not look at the offending food.

The nurse stood firmly with her hands on her hips.

Abby placed the silver cover over the sandwich. "Eew."

Chapter 11

Camera Shy

Nurse Anesthetist Eric was faced with the task of weaning the Chimera from the sedative. All involved were apprehensive.

"There is so much we do not know," said Eric. Will it be fearful? Calm? Aggressive? This is unchartered waters for all of us, the Chimera included."

"The Chimera's restraints will remain," said Dr. Liu. "For now."

Nurse Eric carefully monitored the Chimera while Nurse Vicki removed the feeding tube, and disconnected the respirator. It was no longer sedated, but not exactly alert either. It began to move a bit, on that first day, but spent most of the time asleep.

At the end of the shift, Eric happily left the Sutherland estate for the evening, breathing a sigh of relief as the driveway gates opened. He drove off with the dread of returning to maintain the unknown beast that had become his job. "99% boredom, 1% panic" was the norm in his profession. Eric wondered if in caring for the Chimera, those percentages might just reverse.

On the second day, Nurse Vicki was examining the I.V. port, only to find the Chimera's eyes fully opened, watching her. "Ooh!" She was startled, put her hand over her heart, and jumped back, but the Chimera was not fazed. It did not react. Instead, it calmly looked around the room, and at the medical staff, seemingly without interest or concern.

Staffers were a bit on edge. They were careful never to turn their back to the Chimera, and did their best to watch its every move. All studied the creature, this curious life form, but for what? They did not know. Perhaps, they looked for signs of cognition, personality, or violence.

Day three was fraught with restless fidgeting. The Chimera turned its head constantly, and moved its body in an effort to stretch, or get up from its forced prone position on the gurney. Eric watched the beast in its minor discomfort. He stepped on the electric pedal operating the hospital bed, so that the Chimera's head and torso were raised. He also lifted the wheel locks to their open position, and turned the bed to face the garden.

Nurse Vicki walked in. She had a large baby bottle on a tray. She smiled at Eric. "Feeding time. It must be hungry."

"A bottle?" asked Eric. He watched in amazement as the Chimera greedily emptied what seemed like sixty four ounces of protein fluid in record time.

"Dr. Liu's orders." She put the empty bottle back on the tray. She peeled the blankets back by another twelve inches, revealing the Chimera's deformed appendages, "We aren't sure it can feed itself."

Eric examined it, and nodded in agreement.

"I'm just hoping Dr. Liu doesn't want to remove that catheter anytime soon." She laughed nervously. "If it can't feed itself, how could it? Well, you know." More nervous giggles escaped her.

Day four began with an increasingly unhappy Chimera.

"Squeaaal, squeal, squeal!" The cries boomed so loudly, they were glad that Abby had been moved to the north wing, away from the noise. It thrashed in the bed. The Nurse adjusted the bed, so the Chimera was more upright, but nothing worked. She fed it, still, its agitation grew. Dr. Liu looked in on it, examining the extreme abrasions caused by the Chimera struggling against the restraints.

"Squeaaaal squeal, squeal!" Its cries carried an element of pain, and despair "**Squeaal, squeal, squeal!"**

"Administer .25 milligrams of benzodiazepine. I want it calm, but awake," directed Dr. Liu. Nurse Eric was quick to comply, eager for the constant squealing to stop.

Within a few minutes, the Chimera began to settle. Squeals of dismay were replaced with occasional grunts, and snorts. It stared out the window at the picture perfect day. The nurse watched its eyes follow the tree branches as they swayed in the wind. She thought of her own children, how they loved to be outside, and sighed. "Maybe it doesn't like to be kept indoors all of the time?"

Dr. Liu shook his head. "No. It will stay inside. Until we have a grip on the Chimera's habits and behavior, it isn't going anywhere."

The next morning, the Chimera awoke to a series of violent fits so extreme that it even refused food. The nurse tried to get it to eat, but it thrashed with such a force, her tray was up ended. The protein drink spilled on the floor. Blood now joined the blackened purple bruises where its extremities were fastened.

"Squeaal, squeal, snort squeaaal squeal!"

"Another dose of benzodiazepine?" asked Nurse Eric.

Dr. Liu stood squarely with his fists pressed firmly at his sides.

"Squeaal, squeal, snort squeaaal squeal!"

"I have an idea," said Vicki. She rushed for her phone, opening her picture file. She sat on the bed, at the Chimera's side as it raged. It ignored her and continued to flail and scream.

"Squeaal, squeal, snort squeaaal squeal!"

"Look at this," said Nurse Vicki softly, aiming the photos for the Chimera's view.

Nurse Eric prepared the sedative.

"Squeaal, squeal, snort squeaaal squeal!"

"This is my son, and this is my daughter." Her voice was gentle and calm.

"Squeaal, snort!"

Just as Nurse Eric prepared to load the syringe into the Chimera's I.V., Dr. Liu waved him back. He was captivated with the nurse's actions, and wanted to observe more.

"This is the two of them together, with our dog."

"Snort, snort, snort."

"Here they are on Christmas day. See how happy they are. They are about your age, I think."

The Chimera turned, and looked the nurse in the eye. The first time he seemed to address any of the medical team as an individual. Until now, it had looked at them, but had never made eye contact. The nurse smiled warmly, and held his gaze.

"Here is another one from Christmas. My goodness, look at all of those toys. They had a great time with those"__ she stopped midsentence, and looked at Dr. Liu, with her eyebrows raised.

"Oh, no you don't nurse. I see where you are going with this, and it will never fly. Mr. Sutherland won't have it! Not for a minute!"

"Snort, snort, snort." The Chimera urged her on with the photo montage.

"It is ridiculous, I tell you!" quibbled Dr. Liu. "We can't treat that thing like a child. I'm surprised you would suggest such a thing as toys! Mr. Sutherland would have all of our jobs for this."

Nurse Vicki was happy to comply with the Chimera's request, sharing dozens of pictures while Dr. Liu rationalized. She and the Chimera exchanged warm glances. "You have big beautiful eyes, just like my son," she said with a smile, then brushed the thin, fine hair on its cheeks with her fingertips. "And this is a picture of the *whole family*."

Chapter 12

Operating Expenses

Maxwell shuffled the papers on his desk in preparation for his usual progress meeting with Dr. Liu.

"I have the monthly expenses from my accountant. I'd like to review a few specific items." Maxwell gave a copy of one of the printed sheets to Dr. Liu. "Mind you, it is not necessarily the amount spent, for these things. I just wonder why are you spending my money on this stuff to begin with? Line item 17 for instance."

Dr. Liu's eyes searched for the item in question. He wondered why Mr. Sutherland was suddenly interested in what was being spent. After all, Liu had always been given carte blanche, the best money could buy, but still, Dr. Liu was careful with what he spent, as careful with Mr. Sutherland's money as if it were his own. Always.

"Line item 17. $2,300.00 for early child development toys. Line item 29. $7,500.00 for a treadmill, and stationery bike. Toys? Exercise equipment? My daughter doesn't need this__ any of it." He pushed the stack of bills aside.

"Sir, those items were not purchased for your daughter, but I am convinced she will see benefit from them." Dr. Liu held his ground.

Maxwell sighed deeply. "That's what I thought. You bought this stuff for the Chimera. You are buying toys for a medical device?" Maxwell questioned the logic of such an outrageous sounding thing the minute it left his lips.

"I understand that this might seem unusual, Sir, but please, hear me out. The first day out of sedation, the Chimera was groggy and tired. He did not struggle against his restraints."

"*Its* restraints." Maxwell cut him off with a stern correction.

Dr. Liu nodded in deference. "The second day, *it* was docile, and very curious about its surroundings. By the fifth day, it was highly agitated, and pulling against the buckles. To distract it, the nurse gave it her car keys to play with. The next day, her cell phone. It worked, but that was a short term solution. It is now bloody and bruised. I'm worried that it may cause itself a stress fracture in the future if we do not address the needs of the Chimera. Yes, I insist that exercise is another of those needs. Again, I can't emphasize enough, that this is all being done to ensure the viability of all of the Chimera's organs for the future needs of Abby."

"But toys?"

"Even the hippo at the zoo has a ball to play with, and a pool to swim in. If the intellectual, and physical needs of the Chimera go unmet, my team and I are concerned for the health and safety of the Chimera, and the health of Abby in turn."

Maxwell leaned back in his desk chair. He exhaled in resignation. "Blah! Toys."

Chapter 13
Cooped Up

Abby, dressed in bedclothes was awake, and rearing to go. It was a picture perfect day, and she was ready to play. She pulled the lowest drawer of a bombe' chest open, rifling through her clothes as she went, tossing her wardrobe on the floor at random.

"Young lady, may I ask what you are doing?" Nurse Vicki stood in the doorway, arms crossed, a foot tapping in judgement.

"I'm getting dressed. I want to go out and play!" The child struggled to put on a fresh pair of socks.

"You will do no such thing. Dr. Liu's orders."

"I'm bored!" Abby served up an extended lower lip.

"Pouting 101. You are a quick study, most likely a master at your craft someday."

"It's sooo pretty outside! Pretty please with a margarita on top?"

"What? *A margarita*?"

"Yes, I heard you tell Nurse Eric that you needed one."

A beet red Nurse Vicki delivered a small case to the child. "Here. Play with your dolls. I'll talk to Dr. Liu. If the weather is favorable in the coming days, he may permit you to go outdoors."

"Yay!"

"I said may. I make no promises, Little Miss. It is entirely up to Dr. Liu."

Abby did not reply to Nurse Vicki, as she frantically sorted through her doll case. "Maggie? I can't find Maggie!"

Chapter 14

The New Kid

Abby decided to search her old room on the other side of the vast mansion of Sutherland Knoll. Abby barged in. "Hey, Kid! What are you doing in my old room?"

The Chimera balked, burying its head into the puff of pillows.

"Did you take Maggie? She's my favorite."

"Snort."

Abby noticed the medical equipment, the tubes and wires, she knew well enough to despise. "Are you sick too?"

The Chimera dared not move, only his saucer shaped eyes far too large for his head followed her as she darted around the machines, and under the bed.

"Here she is!" Abby stood at the edge of the bed, stroking the fashion doll's matted hair with her hand. "You want to see her?" Abby jumped on the mattress with the Chimera. She knelt beside him.

The beast glanced at the doll, and then at Abby. He had seen children before, but only in pictures. He grunted, and smiled, exposing an adorable set of perfectly formed baby teeth, too small for his mouth.

"Isn't she pretty?" Abby held the naked doll in need of a hair do for his inspection.

"Snort."

"Hee, hee! You sound like a piggy!"

"Abby! Abby, where are you?"

"Next time you want to play with Maggie, please ask my permission!" Abby nodded at her firm declaration of toy sharing terms, even though it was she who had mistakenly left her doll behind in the first place.

"Abby! Where are you?" Voices of Nurse Vicki, and Dr. Liu were drawing closer.

She jumped from the bed, sticking the landing like a seasoned gymnast.

The Chimera tried to pull her back, keeping her there with him, but the bloodied belts held him firmly to the bed.

"Squeal! Squeal!"

"I'm in big trouble. I have to go!"

Chapter 15

The Great Escape

Abby navigated the grand halls and paneled passageways of the mansion with an ease and quickness rivalling any of the staff on a deadline. She pulled back the bedsheets, and jumped in.

"Don't forget, Maggie, I found you on the closet floor. We have been here the whole time!" Abby forced the doll to nod in agreement. "I think you should wear something pretty," the child put her finger to her chin in careful consideration of Maggie's vast wardrobe options. "Here. How about this blue one?"

Maxwell Sutherland appeared from around the corner. "What do you mean, missing?" he asked. "I am certain I heard her as I walked by just moments ago." He opened the door. "See! I told you as much.

Playing with her dolls. Young lady, have you been out of bed today?"

"Yes, Daddy. I couldn't find Maggie, so I searched all around the room to find her."

"There. That settles it. Next time, take a peek under the bed or in the closet before you call out the National Guard. You had me worried sick. I'll be in my study." Maxwell kissed Abby on the forehead.

Nurse Vicki stood in judgement of the little escape artist. "I spoke to Dr. Liu before your little disappearing act. He agreed that weather permitting, you could go outside, supervised, of course, but now that I have spent the better part of an hour chasing after you, I'll have to catch up on my lost work. Too bad that now I won't have time to take you out. I hear it's to be sunny and eighty degrees. Oh, well, what's one more day of being cooped up in this stuffy old house?"

Abby bit her lower lip, and kept silent. She longed to be outside, but at least she could visit the sick kid in her old room. How nice it would be to finally have someone to play with!

Chapter 16

Agree to Disagree

The next morning, Abby was up, out of bed and dressed without a single article of clothing left on the floor. She sat with Maggie in a fluffy arm chair at the window. Morning sun poured in through the lace curtains.

"You didn't eat your breakfast." Nurse Vicki surveyed the tray.

"I'm not hungry." The doll, Maggie shook her head in agreement with Abby.

"This is the fourth day in a row, and you barely touched dinner. Stand up for me, please."

The child complied. Her clothes were poorly fitted even though she had worn them a few times previously. The waistline of her khaki shorts was so tight it looked as if it would burst open, but her shirt sleeves, and leg openings appeared so large, her little arms and legs were swimming in a sea of extra fabric.

"Come with me. We're going to check your weight."

Abby stepped on the scale.

"Hmm." Nurse Vicki pursed her lips. "I am going to put a collection bin in your toilet bowl. Please don't flush it. I want to send a stool sample to the lab."

"Eeew."

"Ha, ha! Eeew, indeed! Imagine how those lab technicians feel." She scribbled some notes in a medical chart. "Remember, you are to remain inside, today. No funny business, agreed?" asked Nurse Vicki.

"Agreed."

The instant the door closed, and her jailer gone, Abby slid the hand that she kept behind her back for Maggie to inspect, her middle and index fingers, crossed.

Chapter 17

Say My Name

"Psst. Psst. Hey, are you awake?" Abby whispered as she let herself in. The Chimera squirmed, and wiggled to sit upright in the presence of his most distinguished guest. His eyes opened wide to take her in. Hints of white baby teeth could be seen through a thin lipped smile.

"We haven't been properly introduced. Allow me. I'm Abigail Sutherland. My friends call me Abby. What's your name?"

"Snort. Snort."

"You don't have to be shy." Abby took the medical chart from the clip board at the foot of the Chimera's bed, and flipped it open." It says here that your name is Zhū. Zhū? What kind of name is that?"

"Snort."

"Can you talk?" Abby tilted her head and squinted at the Chimera. She pointed at herself in the chest. "I'm Abby. Can you say my name? Ab-by?"

The Chimera's eyes never left her. He moved his mouth, but no sound could be heard.

"Here, like this!" Abby jumped on the bed beside him. She mouthed her name with a deliberate slowness, her face merely inches from his. "Ab-by."

"Bab-by!" declared the Chimera. His voice warbled.

Abby smiled, and kept on trying. "Here, like this! Aaaa." She showed him her tongue, curled behind her lower teeth. "You do it." She placed her soft little hands on either side if his hairy face. He lowered his eyes, turning away, but Abby insisted. She guided his face back toward hers. "Come on, try. Aaaa."

"Aaa."

"Again! Aaa."

"Aaa."

"Ab-by."

"Ab-by." His small voice, the bright treble keys of a piano.

"Zhū-Zhū, you did it!" She threw her arms around him in a celebratory hug.

"Abby, Abby, snort, Abby!"

"Come on! Let's go do something fun, Zhū-Zhū! Let's go outside!" She pulled his top sheet back to take him by the hand, but stopped suddenly.

Zhū cowered at her reaction. His nose twitched, as he looked away.

"Your hands. What happened to__?" She touched his wide, split cloven center fingers, and thick rigid nails, then traced the outline of two smaller digits on either side, resembling her own fingers. Then, she noticed the bloodstained restraints, and his bruised appendages slightly resembling arms.

He winced as she touched the tethers. "Squeal!!"

"I'll bet that hurts! I'm sorry Zhū-Zhū! Here! Let me get you out of those terrible things!"

Abby gently went to work, to free him, but only managed to undo one of the buckles.

"We'll know once the lab gets the sample. Order a PET scan." A familiar voice trailed down the hallway.

"Dr. Liu! He's coming! I have to go!" Abby jumped down from the bed, and disappeared through the

Jack and Jill bathroom, escaping via the service stair at the end of the hall.

"Squeal! Squeal! Squeal!"

Zhū pleaded for her to stay with him, holding an outstretched bristly pink battered arm, but it was no use. He could only hold on to the one thing she left him, her name. "Snort. Snort."

"Abby."

Chapter 18

Pinky Swear

Nurse Vicki pulled the drapery open, streams of sunshine kissed Abby's cheeks. "Wake up, sleepy head. It's nearly ten. You don't want to sleep away a beautiful day like this one, do you?"

A groggy Abby rubbed her eyes, and picked the grit of sleep with her thumb and forefinger.

"Here's your breakfast. The cook has been keeping it warm for you all morning." A bamboo tray with sterling silver fittings was placed in front of the girl.

"But I'm too tired to eat." Abby sat up, arms crossed in what had become her standard meal-time protest.

"Oh, that's terrible. If you are too tired to eat, then going outside today is out of the question. The staff was just setting the cushions out under the pergola for you. I'll just tell them to never mind."

"Outside? Really? Pinky swear?"

Nurse Vicki stood over the child. Her eyes narrowed. "Only if you eat your breakfast."

"Deal!"

The two hooked their fingers in solemn agreement.

The cover was removed from the plate to reveal a poached egg, bacon, and skinned and seeded grapefruit sections in a small crystal compote.

"B- bacon?" The salty sweet hickory aroma wafted towards Abby's face. She gulped, and exhaled in an effort to clear her nostrils from an ungodly stench. She took another small breath, with her head turned away from the meal, but it was no use. The child began to heave.

Choke! Spit!

Abby ran to the bathroom as quickly as she could, overturning the tray that came crashing to the floor.

Chapter 19

The Blues King

Nurse Vicki dutifully cleaned Abby up, and dressed her for the day.

"Since breakfast was a no-go, I have asked the kitchen to send a chocolate protein drink out to the pergola for you. I want you to promise me that you'll drink the whole thing, okay?"

Abby nodded in agreement, her throat still raw from the vomit. She pitifully looked up at Nurse Vicki with yellowed eyes, and lethargically took Vicki's hand.

It was a beautiful day, despite the rocky start for Abby. The skies were clear, and the typical humidity of an east coast summer was nonexistent. Abby, clinging to a stylishly attired Maggie took refuge in a wide French style chair, the seat, so deep, that her dimpled ankles barely hung over the edge. She settled in, and sipped her protein shake, contended by the view.

"My, it is so beautiful out here. I understand why you love it so much," marveled Nurse Vicki, as she touched the flowering tangerine trumpet of a climbing vine. Cheery dots of spicy scented blooms nodded overhead, woven on the trellis.

"That's Madame Galen! She is pretty." Abby took a lingering breath. "Smells pretty too!"

"The vine has a name?"

"Yes. Daddy told me her name. He said that my mother planted it just before I was born."

Abby looked up through the blooms as she sipped. Her ankles turning her sandaled feet in tune with a distant melody only she could hear.

Buzz. Buzz.

Nurse Vicki checked her messages. "A text from Dr. Liu. He is at the lab. He wants to see me right away."

"Aww, do I have to go back inside?" Abby crinkled her nose as she pouted. Her feet still dancing away.

"Well, you have had a nasty morning. I think the fresh air will do you some good. I should be only a few minutes."

"Yay! Oh, thank you! I knew you'd let me stay."

"Remember our bargain. Finish that drink!"

Abby sat sipping her cleverly disguised nutritional supplement.

"Sluuurrp! Aah!"

She let out a burp with the last of the glass. For a moment, she was quiet, and content, but when one is eight years old, moments are but an excruciating eternity.

From where she sat under the pergola, Abby could see the doors of her former bedroom were open wide. Enticed by the opportunity to see her new friend, Abby climbed out of the bergere, bid farewell to Madame Galen, and skipped off to pay a visit.

"You first, Maggie, see if the coast is clear."

The tiny rubber head of the fashion doll peered around the swaying drapery.

Zhū failed to notice.

"Is it safe?"

Maggie nodded a full body gesture of affirmation.

Zhū sniffed the air, his bright pink nostrils snotty and quivering.

The head of Maggie, and her best gal pal peeked in.

"Bab-by!" exclaimed Zhū with a grunt.

Abby let herself in. "No, no, no! It's Abby, remember? Let's try it again!" She jumped on the bed beside him, with her face to his, mouth open wide, again, demonstrating tongue placement. He gleefully mimicked her.

"Aaa."

"Baa."

"Try it again! Aaa."

"Aaa. Abby!"

"Yes! You have it! I'm sure you just had a temporary lapse."

Zhū smiled and snorted. Abby was back!

"Zhū-Zhū, I have the bestest idea! It's a perfect day. Let's go to the stables, I haven't seen my horse in an awful long time, and you can meet him. Why are you just sitting there, let's go!" She threw the sheet back to see that he was once again, tied to the bed. "This is mean! I don't like these. Here, I'm taking these off. Hold still."

The bruises on his stubby arms were worse in number and severity. She was careful not to hurt the blackish yellow tinted sores as she worked to free him.

"There. That's better. Let's go."

Zhū stayed silent, pointing to the foot of the bed where he lay. He worked the sheet away with his cloven hoofed hands. His feet, a more elongated version of his malformed pointers were also bound.

"Woah! Your feet too? They look as strange as your hands! Boy, you are one weird looking kid, Zhū-Zhū." She crocked an eyebrow. "Hey, are you from New Jersey?"

Finally, Zhū was unrestrained. Abby used all of her might to help him sit and then stand under his own power. He wobbled around the room before righting himself. His knees knocked together, and his posture was rounded at the shoulder, hunched like a brittle boned octogenarian.

"Pants!" Abby exclaimed when she noticed the exposed dimply rump through the slit in Zhū's hospital gown. She climbed to the top of a white metal counter to the side of the room, pulling out a bright blue pair of scrubs. "Here. These should fit."

Zhū stood, leaning against the bed for stability, unsure what exactly he was supposed to do with the ball of blue fabric.

"Here, like this." Abby helped him into the scrubs. She pulled the waistband up, stopping at Zhū's mid-thigh. "You should pull them up to your waist by yourself. Careful, don't twist your winkie in the elastic."

The puzzled beast caulked his head.

"Snort. Snort."

"Your winkie, you know," she pointed at his crotch. "It's not that big of a deal. Just the thing that makes you a boy, that's all."

Did it matter if Zhū understood her words and gestures? To him, it did not. It wasn't what she said, while gleefully flapping about, but it delighted him instead, in how she said it, and most important to Zhū, was that whatever she said, she was saying it *to him*.

The journey to the stables was a long one. The boost of energy Abby enjoyed from the protein drink was fading. Without benefit of exercise equipment handles, or straps to hold on to, Zhū labored to keep his balance walking upright.

Abby rolled the massive stable door open. Zhū jumped back.

"Squeal! Squeal!"

"It's okay, Zhū-Zhū." She patted his hand to console him. Every hair on his body stood to her gentle touch. "These are horses. That black and white one is mine. His name is Fats Domino Blues King. I just call him Dom. Someday, when I'm all better, I'm going to ride him. Daddy promised I could. Do you want to pet him?"

Before Zhū could evaluate the situation, Abby was pulling him to Dom's stall. Abby fed Dom an apple, which he took gingerly from the girl's hand.

"Here, you try."

Abby handed Zhū an apple, but he struggled to hold it for the deformity of his hybridized hands. The apple rolled to the ground, inside the stall, at Dom's shoed hoof. Zhū knelt to retrieve it, taking note of the similarity of Dom's hooves, and his own hands. He studied them, side by side for an instant, but a greedy Dom bent down and snatched the apple. As the hungry equine chewed, Zhū touched its ears, and then his own. Again, he found a striking similarity in both shape and texture.

A single tear fell down his stubbly cheek. Zhū knew little of this world that he had been unwittingly thrust into. He knew only that he was a stranger, a product not only of another place, but an invader being neither man nor beast. Zhū understood that he was both, therefore, he was all things, and yet, nothing.

"Don't cry, Zhū-Zhū." Abby brushed his cheek. I know Dom is big, and can be kinda scary, but he really is gentle, I promise."

Zhū's eyes held hers, and that sweet, sincere little face that he lived for.

"Abby?"

"Yes, Zhū-Zhū?"

His watery eyes pleaded with her, as he motioned toward the door. He reached for her hand.

"Okay, we can leave. Bye Dom!"

Chapter 20

Off With Their Heads

"Not good news, is it?" asked Nurse Vicki.

"You know I never enjoy a nurse that chooses to diagnose, but your suspicions were correct," said Dr. Liu.

Nurse Vicki exhaled through pursed lips as she stared at the ceiling. "Poor kid. What good is it to be born with a silver spoon, when you are fed by an IV? If it isn't one thing, it's another. Stage?"

"Stage two, it is early, but we have to move fast to give her a chance to beat this thing."

CRNA Eric burst into the lab. "He's missing! The Chimera! He's gone!"

"But how?" asked Liu.

"I don't know." Eric shrugged.

All three raced to the room where Zhū spent his days. Nurse Eric kept talking.

"It was time to start a new round of anesthesia. I prepped, but when I got to the patient, see! The bed is empty!"

Together, they scoured the room for their missing multimillion dollar medical device. Eric peered into the closet, Dr. Liu, the bathroom, Nurse Vicki, under the bed. She balled up the sheets in frustration, noting the unbuckled tethers, but then it fell to the floor at her feet, clear cut evidence of an inside job.

Maggie.

Vicki held the doll up for the others to see. "Looks like the Chimera has an accomplice."

Maxwell Sutherland tapped at the door before letting himself in. "Dr. Liu, I'd like to see you about the quarterly__what's this? Where is the Chimera?"

"Given the limited range of his vestigial digits, he couldn't have left on his own. We think that Abby may have unleashed the Chimera," said Liu.

"We'll discuss specifics later," said Maxwell Sutherland. "I think I know where to find them. If any harm has come to my daughter. Heads will roll!"

Chapter 21

Hide and Seek

Maxwell and Nurse Vicki crested the hill to the Sutherland's stables. The building, a far cry from a barn. In the waning sunlight, the massive structure seemed more a chateaux than shed. The limestone structure with copper mansard roofline, and leaded glass windows called to the rich, comforting them with all the luxury both familiar, and required. The pair gasped for breath at the summit.

"You. Check the stalls, I'll search the track and neighboring pasture," commanded Maxwell.

Nurse Vicki walked down the center hall, eyes scanning everything. This horse pen was as grand a place as any she had seen on television. The wrought iron chandeliers and matching sconces were by her estimation, more expensive than her car. Still, she concentrated on her task, to find Abby, and the Chimera, both unharmed, thus saving her own livelihood, and posterior.

One arched pen after another revealed nothing but millions in horseflesh, and zero in finding her charge. Vicki made her way down the long, covered loggia. Maxwell stood, stoic, with his hands in his hair.

Vicki followed his line of sight.

In a bale of new mown hay, lay his baby, Abby, the only thing he had left in the world to live for. She was lying side by side, spooning with the monster he bought to save her life.

With great haste, Maxwell ran into the stable, accosted the first stable boy he saw and wrested the shovel from his hands, as the lad worked, mucking the stalls.

"Give me that!"

Vicki looked over her shoulder, unsure of what Mr. Sutherland would do, and equally hesitant of what she should do.

Abby and Zhū seemed to stir from the bucolic bliss that was their nap. Both were covered in mud stained clothing, a tell-tale indication of how they played, rolling in the deep dirty puddles in order to cool off. Maxwell became more enraged as the Chimera buried his nose in Abby's dirty tangled hair. Zhū's eyes fluttered open in the shade of a towering Maxwell Sutherland. Zhū smiled his chicklet toothed smile, pulling his beloved closer to him, he said his favorite word.

"Abby."

"You! You ungodly beast! You leave her alone!"

Abby rubbed her eyes as Maxwell raised the shovel overhead.

Chapter 22

A Statement of Fact

The office was in complete disarray. Chairs were overturned. Drapery was torn from their rods, reduced to crumpled balls of silk on the floor. The trio stepped gingerly over an island chain of books with pages torn, and bindings bent.

Dr. Liu, and Nurses Vicki and Eric stood quivering at the desk of Maxwell Sutherland. Their eyes darted, tracing the curvilinear pattern of the Oriental rug at their feet, or at each other, but none dared to make eye contact with their huffing, red faced employer.

Maxwell dabbed his brow with a lightly starched white handkerchief before filling his pipe with a custom tobacco blend of Syrian latakia and perique, the concoction he used to help himself relax. The temper tantrum of destroying his own office served only to take the edge off of his fury. He clicked the silver lighter shaped like a suit of armor, and languidly puffed away, fading into his desk chair. On any other day, he would have offered them a comfy perch on one of the many deeply tufted seats. After finding his only daughter in the arms of the freak, the monster miracle of science, created for the sole purpose of saving her fragile life, he realized that it was not an ordinary day. He would not treat it as such.

"Mr. Sutherland, Sir, It is all my fault," confessed Nurse Vicki. "I was needed at the lab. She was on the patio, under the pergola, smiling and happy, enjoying this beautiful day. I didn't have the heart to disturb her. It was only a few minutes."

Maxwell puffed, brooded, and listened through his thick filter of anger. He exhaled a thin white cloud, and laid the spent bowl in the crystal ashtray.

"I don't take negligence lightly, Nurse, especially when the welfare of Abby is concerned. Do you have children?"

"I do."

Maxwell raised his eyebrows. "Well then, you of all people should share my apprehension. You must care for Abby as you would your own." He tapped the embers into the dish, and packed a second pipe. "That is not just my expectation. It is my requirement. That said, I am a firm believer that it is never wise to change a horse mid-stream."

Nurse Vicki shed part of her worry about being terminated, until Maxwell began to speak again.

"Abby is quite dependent on you, Nurse, both physically and emotionally. I don't wish to take that from her. The child has lost too much already. It is for that reason, I have decided that the Chimera must be moved to an offsite location at once. Dr. Liu, see to it as soon as possible."

"Mr. Sutherland, Sir, I don't think that is wise given the latest developments." While Maxwell bristled, Dr. Liu opened a manila folder, placing it carefully on the desk for him to read. "It was brought to my attention by Nurse Vicki. It is she who noticed the rapid weight loss, and chalky stools. That is why Nurse Vicki was absent from Abby. I sent for her, to review the lab's findings. You see, Sir, moving the Chimera now would put Abby's life in jeopardy."

Maxwell searched each page of the file, as the blood of anger drained from his face turning him hauntingly pale. He slumped in his chair, a man defeated.

"Liver cancer? Stage 2? What is your proposed course of action?"

"Removal of all diseased tissue, and a partial transplant from the Chimera. It is tricky, true, especially given the advanced development of the cells, but I think our team can pull it off."

"Wait! What?" Vicki's head was reeling. "Do you mean to tell me that we are still going to treat the Chimera like some inanimate object? Even after what we all just witnessed?"

"Now see here Nurse! My patience is already worn thin with your latest dereliction of duty. You are here to take care of Abby! If there is some reason why you are unable to take orders on her behalf, you are free to go. No doubt your family can't afford an unemployed mother, especially one who won't find another job in healthcare."

"Am I being threatened?"

"Absolutely not, Nurse. I make no threats. It is merely a statement of fact."

"But he's smart! You all heard him! He can speak! He said Abby's name!"

"Need I remind you, Nurse," Maxwell's eyes laden with contempt pierced her, "that the Chimera is a *medical device*, one that will be used in any capacity necessary to keep my Abby alive. As for intelligence? Speech? On your way back to Abby, I'd suggest you peek into the conservatory. I have a pair of African Gray Parrots that can sing the National Anthem."

Chapter 23

Outdoor Plumbing

"I want to see him!" cried Abby.

"Let's have a look at those stitches. Abby, hold still, please!"

"I'm fine! Please, let me see him!"

Nurse Vicki held the dressing in one hand, wiggled her eyebrows, and gave the girl a goofy sideways smile that always worked on dissolving Abby's stubborn streaks.

With lips pursed, and a deep breath, the child surrendered to an uneasy truce with Nurse Vicki. She lifted her gown, showing a horizontal arc that ran the entire width of her abdomen, just below her ribs. Her incision was healing nicely, considering the size.

"Well, this looks pretty good. No sign of infection. Now remember, you mustn't strain yourself. No monkey business, okay?"

"Define monkey business."

"You know perfectly well what I mean. Dr. Liu wants you to stay in bed and rest, so that you can heal. Your body has been through a lot."

"But I want to see him!"

"Good morning, Mr. Sutherland. I didn't see you come in." Vicki drew back the curtain. You'll be happy to see that our little patient has come through the partial liver transplant beautifully."

"Yes, Nurse, Dr. Liu has briefed me on Abby's condition." Maxwell made a bee line for the hospital bed where his daughter recovered. "Ah, Princess Abby! Good morning!" Maxwell ran his fingers through her baby fine hair.

The girl screwed her face into a contorted mixture of anger and avoidance. She turned her head away, and squeezed her eyes shut tight. Maxwell's hand hen brushed her cheek, but she refused to acknowledge him.

"Aren't you going to wish me a good morning?" nudged Maxwell.

"No. I'm not talking to you, Daddy." Abby huffed. "I'm mad at you! You hurt Zhū-Zhū! You are mean!" Tears formed in the corners of her eyes as she began to snivel and cry.

"Oh, Abby, Baby, Don't you understand that I was just trying to protect you? If that thing harmed you, I'd never forgive myself."

Abby opened her eyes, her tenuous wall of silence, crumbled. "I'm not a baby! I'm a big girl, Daddy! Zhū-Zhū would never hurt me. (Sniff.) He's my friend!"

It was now Maxwell's turn to purse his lips and turn away. He sat on the edge of the bed, and selected his words one by one. "Abby, honey." He held her sweet, angelic face in his hands. "I need you to listen carefully, and know that I want nothing but the best for you. You know that, don't you?"

Abby nodded.

"That's my good girl. That thing is not your friend. It is very strong, and it could hurt you very badly."

"But Daddy," Abby wiped her eyes on the back of her hand. "Don't take him away from me! Zhū-Zhū is my only friend!"

"Only friend? What am I, chopped liver?" Nurse Vicki piped up, and offered a box of tissues.

Abby blew her nose, and forced a smile that ended in a yawn. "No liver jokes, please."

Maxwell calmly held his finger to her lips. "Shhh. I realize, Abby, that it is sometimes lonely, that you miss being around children your own age, but I promise, once you're better, we'll fix that okay? In the meantime, you must stay away from that thing."

Abby squirmed to make herself comfortable. She wanted so badly to argue, but weariness crept over her. Her voice softened to a pitch just above a whisper.

"Daddy, Zhū-Zhū isn't a thing. He's a boy. He has a winkie and everything."

"A what?" Maxwell's eyes bulged out of their sockets. "Never mind, I heard you. What do you know about such things?"

"You know, Daddy. Boy parts. Zhū-Zhū has boy parts. I saw it. He's different than girls. Nurse Vicki explained it all to me."

"Oh she did, did she?" Maxwell seemed to triple in size with his hands on his hips. His eyes burned holes through Nurse Vicki's scrubs.

Vicki panicked, sending an entire tray of syringes and pills crashing to the floor. She flushed with embarrassment, but was grateful for an excuse to escape the ire of Maxwell Sutherland.

"You see, it's very simple, Daddy. It's really just a matter of indoor, or outdoor plumbing."

Chapter 24

Mutiny

Vicki examined the basin used to catch the latest stool sample from Abby. The whitish tell tale sign of liver cancer was gone, only to be replaced by a strong streak of crimson.

"Blood. Lots of it. Why can't this kid catch a break?"

"The disease has traveled to her colon. I was afraid of that," said Dr. Liu, as he closed the file. "I ordered a RAS test as well. It is metastatic, no mutation."

"Okay, I like good news. That means that it is treatable with chemo, like cancer, right?" asked Vicki.

"Nurse Vicki, Eric, walk with me for a minute."

The two followed Dr. Liu through the long corridor that connected the surgical wing of the Sutherland Mansion to the rest of the house. Liu opened a pair of French doors that led to a geometry of boxwood hedges and a bronze fountain of dancing nymphs. It was still early. The cool dew of morning had yet to lift.

"I'm afraid the walls have ears, so to speak," began Liu. "In answer to your question, Nurse Vicki, yes. This mirrors a type of colon cancer that is common. Chemotherapy would be a natural choice, but let us not forget that Abby has only one kidney, and is recuperating from a partial liver transplant."

"So what can be done for her? We can't just sit on our hands. There must be something, another surgery?" mused Vicki.

"Unfortunately, there is no perfect answer. There are tremendous risks for Abby either way. If I administer dialysis, she may be able to filter the infusions. I have thought long and hard about the proper course of action, that is why I have asked you two out here. I would like to start chemotherapy immediately, *without* the knowledge of Mr. Sutherland."

"You want to *what?* I don't know about this," objected Eric. "We are on thin ice with Mr. Sutherland as it is."

"Why the secrecy? Mr. Sutherland has been kept up to date of the most inconsequential details, and this is a big deal," Vicki chimed in.

"My concern that Mr. Sutherland will demand surgery the minute he learns of Abby's latest diagnosis. She has just been through too much. This latest development comes way too soon. As for the Chimera, he, uh, I mean *it* is healing well enough, but I see other changes that I find concerning. Please, look in on the Chimera for yourselves. You'll see what I mean. If you agree that we should proceed with the chemotherapy, without Mr. Sutherland's knowledge, we will have to stay united as a team."

"A team? Up until now, Dr. Liu, you have been in lockstep with Mr. Sutherland's wishes. Why the sudden desire for insubordination?"

"He does have a good point," added Vicki.

Dr. Liu put his hands in the pockets of his white coat. "No, no. I think that's a fair question. My 'desire for insubordination' as you put it, Eric is nothing more than a choice to do what is best. I took this job because I was dedicated to saving Abby Sutherland's life. I also took an oath to do no harm. Surgery at this time in my opinion, does harm to both Abby *and* the Chimera. After what I witnessed with Mr. Sutherland's shovel assault on the Chimera, I no longer think that he is a man that can see reason in this situation. I am concerned that all of us are in well over our heads. That is why I hope that we will proceed as a team. Our goal is to bring no harm to each other, or our patients, both of them."

"We'll all lose our licenses, let alone our jobs! There is no way! How can we keep Mr. Sutherland from knowing about this?" asked Eric as he shuffled his feet over the creamy travertine pavers.

"This is Mr. Sutherland's busiest time of year, a time when he travels extensively for business. The first leg of his trip has him in the Pacific Rim for ten days, after that, Brussels. That gives us the opportunity to administer one round. I can evaluate her progress from there. One round, that's all I ask. If the two of you treat the Chimera, and agree with me, then we will proceed, if not, it is inevitable that both Abby and the Chimera will go into surgery immediately." Dr. Liu checked his watch. "I'll expect your answers by noon, today. We will only proceed with chemotherapy if our decision to do so is unanimous."

Chapter 25

A Broken Heart

It was a curious thing, this living, breathing bag of bologna pink flesh, for its conundrum of beauty and repugnance, self-possession and servitude, for its physical strength, and powerlessness. The beast arrived an innocent, at the peak of life that was slowly being drained, and an intelligence that his captors dared not cultivate, or cared not to understand, save one, little Abby Sutherland. Abby, the one person the Chimera lived for, was the very thing he was denied.

The dressing was pulled back from the sutures. The scar was healed, as had been the case with every procedure the Chimera was forced to endure. The wound, clean as it was, only highlighted the Chimera's deeper scars.

Nurse Vicki went about her tasks for the morning, paying special attention to the Chimera's condition, as Dr. Liu suggested. The Dr. was right, there were changes. She unfastened the restraints, but the Chimera did not struggle. As she checked his bruises where Mr. Sutherland's shovel made contact, she found his once taught skin, hide, whatever it was, to be sagging, and wrinkled. The dark, bristly patches of hair around his nose and ears were suddenly peppered with gray. As she checked his vitals, Zhū made no reaction, or attempt to engage her. His eyes were vacant, his breath, metered, but shallow. She pulled a tray of food to him, but Zhū showed no interest in that either.

Vicki pulled out her cell phone, and laid it on the tray table in front of Zhū. The screen showed a picture of Abby, taken just before the liver surgery. She was lounging in a deep chair under the pergola. Rays of sunshine streamed through the vines of trumpet flowers, kissing her freckled cheeks.

"Snort. Snort."

"She is very sick again, or should I say still? We're going to try to help her with medicine."

"Nurse, does that mean you have made a decision?" interrupted Dr. Liu.

Nurse Vicki nudged close to Dr. Liu, away from the Chimera's ear shot. She funneled her words with her hand. "Yes, I agree with you. He is changed," she whispered. "It's almost as if he is dying, __ of a broken heart. Yes. I think we should proceed as a team."

"A smaller team, I'm afraid. Nurse Eric just tenured his resignation."

"Eric, is that true?"

"I'm sorry." Eric shouldered a sack containing his belongings as two members of security stood at the treatment room door. They waited to escort him off the property. "This is all way too weird for me."

As Eric walked away, Vicki wondered how they could proceed without a crucial team member. "This is bad."

"To the contrary, this is perfect. It will take me weeks to replace him, at best. I will notify Mr. Sutherland of Abby's condition, and Eric's resignation. Given the circumstances, we cannot perform surgery without a CRNA, so we will have no option but chemotherapy until our staffing issues are resolved."

"What about a public hospital? They have the staff and the facilities."

"Are you forgetting something, Nurse?" Dr. Liu motioned with his pen toward the Chimera. "Mr. Sutherland would never allow it."

"When do we start chemotherapy?"

"I have a meeting with Mr. Sutherland before his flight to Singapore. Once I have his consent, we'll get moving." Dr. Liu checked his watch, and left the room.

Chapter 26

A Horse Race

"Bring the monitor to Abby. I want to talk to my daughter."

Nurse Vicki propped the lap top open on top of a tray table in front of Abby. The girl's face was swollen with a fiery red rash rivaled only by her teary, blood shot eyes. Her inflated face, barely recognizable to her own father. Maxwell Sutherland winced, then blinked the reality that was his daughter's condition into focus. He was visibly startled, but did his best to smooth it over, and behave as if everything was perfectly fine. The poker face he had learned in the business world was only a tattered veil in the face of Abby's latest trial.

"Daddy?"

"Hello, baby girl, yes, it's Daddy." Maxwell smiled into the monitor. "Ah, it is so good to see you. I miss you so much." His voice cracked. "I'm so sorry I can't be there with you right now, but Dr. Liu says that you have been very brave. I'm so proud of you. Tell me, how are you feeling?"

"Okay." Abby's eyes were heavy as her words.

"Oh, sweetheart. I know you are tired. I just had to see you, to tell you that I love you, and that I'll be home as soon as I can. Don't you worry, I'll be there before you know it. The monitor squaked. "Liu, I'd like to continue this call with you in private."

Dr. Liu closed the door to his private office, and placed the lap top down on his desktop alongside a thick stack of charts.

Nurse Vicki took the opportunity to duck out of the room, She made her way to the Chimera.

"You have very little time to go to her." Vicki enticed Zhū with a beckoning index finger. "Abby is very sick. It may be a long time before you get the chance to see her again."

"Snort. Abby? Snort. Snort."

"At the end of the hall, the last room."

"Snort. Snort".

Nurse Vicki slipped away, confident that the Chimera was smart, and understood enough to find

Abby on his own, or at least sniff her out like a prized Perigord truffle. For as much as she wanted to help, this was all she could do. She had already gone too far. From the safety of an adjoining corridor, Vicki watched Zhū wobble his way to the recovery room where Abby lay. She smiled as he wiggled his full torso through the crack in the partially open door. His hoofed feet slid a bit, unable to gain traction on the mirror gloss of the floors.

He staggered across the room as murmurs of an argument emanated from Dr. Liu's office. Zhū sat at her bedside, a bit frightened by all he saw. He knew what the bleeps and machines meant for him, but seeing Abby endure the same made him snivel. He let out a small squeal of remorse.

"Zhū-Zhū?" Abby's sleep laden eyes squinted to focus. "I knew you'd come."

"Snort. Snort." The beast's wide, porcine nostrils twitched. He could smell it. Blood. More specifically, he knew that it was Abby's blood. Zhū ached with the realization of what was to come, for him and Abby both. He bowed his head so that Abby might not see the glint of a tear in the corner of his eye.

The voice of an irate Maxwell Sutherland leaked out under the closed door. "What the hell have you done to her? Abby looks like death warmed over!" The Chimera bristled at Maxwell's voice, the sound that brought him both physical and emotional pain, no matter how squeaky or distant it seemed. The beast cowered, and began to tremble.

"I'll get better soon, you'll see. Then we can run, and play outside." Abby's voice trailed off as the battle behind closed doors swelled. She reached out for him, her arm too weak and tired to stay aloft, fell to the mattress.

Nurse Vicki peeked in. Zhū had snuggled on the edge of the bed. He and Abby were locked in a tight embrace. "Zhū," Vicki whispered. "You must get back to your room now."

Abby hugged him tighter. Her tears fell on the snaps of his hospital gown.

"Abby, Zhū has to go now, or we will all be in big trouble, okay?"

"Okay." Abby sniffed.

The voices of Dr. Liu, and Maxwell Sutherland swelled on the other side of the door.

"I did exactly what I said, following chemotherapy protocols to a T." Liu tried to remain calm in the face of being unduly chastised by Maxwell Sutherland.

"You have obviously dropped the ball somewhere. I'll not stand for it!" The raging conflict, was now far from private.

Zhū stood, and teetered on feet too small for his ample frame. His wet jowls were stained with tears. Nurse Vicki led him away.

"Squeal. Squeal!"

"What was that noise?" demanded Maxwell.

"Noise? I did not hear anything." Liu denied the fact that he had heard every word spoken, __ and snorted in Abby's room, then he persisted with his defense. "Need I remind you, Sir, that Abby is a transplant recipient with a compromised liver, *and* one kidney?"

"Don't get smart with me. Liu. I am fully aware of Abby's condition."

"Chemotherapy is demanding for otherwise healthy people. Unfortunately, Abby is not remotely close to healthy. She is having severe side effects from the chemotherapy. Side effects that we are doing the utmost to treat, but we can no longer continue this course of treatment."

"No more chemo? Why?"

Dr. Liu sat in his desk chair, too exhausted to remain standing for Mr. Sutherland's interrogation. He took off his glasses, resting them in his breast pocket, and melted in the welcoming upholstery.

"Her electrolytes are all low. Liver enzymes? Not good there either. I am sure that you noticed the rash?"

"Of course I noticed! My beautiful baby girl looks like a circus freak thanks to you!"

"Pardon me?"

"Damn it, Liu! You heard me! My Daughter is suffering because of your negligence! I have a good mind to send you packing, but I__"

"You don't change horses mid-stream?" Dr. Liu mocked a man he once respected, but his feelings changed after the shovel incident attacking Zhū at the stables. To the eyes of Dr. Liu, Maxwell Sutherland was quickly showing himself to be a selfish bully, and a bore.

"Don't dare test me. I thought that you were the best, but that obviously is not true! Not only have you not kept Abby's disease in check, you haven't even been able to hold your own staff together. How long until you resolve the staffing issues and can get on with the colectomy?"

"Mr. Sutherland. I *am* the qualified surgeon you believed me to be, and that I am completely devoted to Abby's care."

"Answer the blasted question! How long?"

"As for Anesthesiology, I have a new Doctor, and CRNA in the middle of the background checks. That should be a few more weeks, then, I'll need a gastrointestinal specialist as consult. Best case scenario?" Dr. Liu rubbed his chin as he considered the intricate pieces of the surgical group puzzle. "Six weeks."

"You have two weeks."

"Two weeks! How am I supposed to do that?"

"Double the signing bonus, money makes all things possible!" The computer screen went black.

Dr. Liu leaned back in his chair.

"No, not quite all."

Chapter 27

Options

"But Daddy, I don't want another surgery!"

"Don't just stand there like a dolt, Nurse! Get my daughter a box of tissues!"

Nurse Vicki was scolded again, but she wasn't sure why. Lately, Maxwell Sutherland had taken to the habit of shouting orders, and demeaning everyone. His behavior deteriorated since his most recent business trip abroad. No one could escape his coarse demeanor. She stepped forward to hand the girl a box of fluffy white tear catchers, only to have Maxwell snatch them out of her hand.

"Give me that!" He put a few to Abby's red, sniffling nose. "Blow. That's a good girl. Now you listen to me, Abby. You are one very sick girl. I have moved Heaven and Earth to bring the best of care to you. The least you could do is show a little gratitude. You are having the colectomy, and that's final!"

Abby allowed her body to settle into the billowy softness of her bed, while secretly hoping that the pillows would suck her into a place where there was no sickness and surgery, a place where her father smiled again. She knew he always smiled when things went her father's way, so she nodded in capitulation.

The new nurse anesthetist entered the room, brushing by Vicki as if she was invisible. "Mr. Sutherland, the transplant team would like to review the IPAA, and J pouch options for the Chimera."

Nurse Vicki shot bolts of deadly lightening from her eyes. "I think it is best, nurse to speak to Mr. Sutherland in his office." Her eyes shifted in Abby's direction.

"Tell me what's wrong with my friend! I want to see him!" Abby began to sniffle and cry.

"Never mind, Abby. There is nothing wrong. You get some rest while I have a nice talk with your Doctors," said Maxwell.

Chapter 28

Taking the Lead

Nurse Vicki checked the calendar on her computer screen. "Dr. Liu hasn't scheduled anything. Who called this pre-surgical meeting?"

"Dr. Cantowicz, the team lead, scheduled the meeting. Didn't you get the memo?" The new nurse smirked at Vicki.

"Team lead? He is a new hire! Since when is Cantowicz team lead?" asked Vicki, her hands firmly on her hips.

"You!" Maxwell pointed at Nurse Vicki. "You have upset my daughter. Get Liu on the horn. I want him in my office in thirty minutes!"

Maxwell sped down the series of corridors so quickly, his Italian leather shoes barely touched the gleaming floor boards. He settled in the sanctuary of his office, and waited for Dr. Liu to arrive with a full pipe, and frayed nerves.

Tap. Tap. Tap.

"You wanted to see me?"

"Liu. Yes. Close the door. I'll cut to the chase. You have a mutiny on your hands. Cantowicz and his team are gunning for you. Personally, I don't care if they replace you or not, but I do care about Abby. I'm not going to have factions at war during Abby's surgery. Get control of the team, immediately. Do I make myself clear?"

"Crystal."

"Good. I want you to bump up the surgery. I want it done yesterday!"

"But, Mr. Sutherland, in Abby's current condition, I don't recommend__"

"No buts! You heard me! Don't let the door hit you on the way out."

Chapter 29

Trivial and Trivia

Chilly as the surgical suite was, it was a welcome retreat from the heated exchanges between staff members both old and new. Doctors Liu and Cantowicz stood at the sinks, elbow deep in antimicrobial solution and mutual resentment. Everyone avoided eye contact in the awkward uneasiness of two staggering egos battling for control of Abby and Zhū's future, as they accidentally on purpose elbowed each other as they scrubbed up.

The two patients were prepared for surgery. Abby and Zhū lay unconscious separated by Maxwell Sutherland, the walls of the adjoining surgical rooms, and two teams of brilliant but combative doctors.

"There is one thing I don't understand," said Vicki. "How is it that the Chimera was made with Abby's DNA, but never shows any sign of this malady?"

Dr. Liu adjusted his protective eyewear. "You can credit its pig DNA. Pigs, well, with the exception of a pot belly variety don't get cancer. The rare cases that have been documented have been limited to melanoma."

Vicki pursed her lip considering the new information. "Interesting."

The harvesting process was in full swing in the OR next door. Cauterization of Zhū's abundant and tough connective tissue produced the smell of burning bacon, and singed flesh. It clouded the air as Dr. Cantowicz's team gasped for breath.

Chapter 30

In the Nick of Time

Soft rock from the 1970's played in the background, but there was nothing mellow in the proceedings. During the collection of Zhū's entire large intestine, Nurse Vicki acted as liaison between the busy groups, traversing both rooms as needed. Finally, she wheeled a cart containing their awaited delivery to Dr. Liu. She choked to clear the stench from her lungs, but found the odor so powerful, she could taste it in the back of her mouth. She gagged, and placed the cart containing the large intestine formerly belonging to Zhū to the side.

"Looks like they are about to start on the stoma, and J-Pouch next door," said Vicki.

"It is about time," said Liu.

"She's losing a lot of blood!" shouted a new Dr. "Suction! I said suction, I can't see a damned thing!"

"BP is dangerously low!" said Vicki.

"It's the hepatic artery! You've nicked it!" Dr. Liu pushed one of the most recent hires aside. "Incompetent fool!"

Vicki stood by Liu as he frantically stopped the bleeder, and proceeded to transplant Zhū's large intestine to the cavity where Abby's diseased organ had been removed.

Chapter 31

Short Cuts

"Rough Day?" asked a freshly showered and dressed Cantowicz, as he pulled the doors to the locker room open wide.

From his seated position on the floor, Dr. Liu turned his head slightly. He addressed a snarky and sarcastic Cantowicz through the opening between his arm and his knees, where his head rested. He was just too tired to lift it.

"How is it you are already finished?"

"That's just how the pros do it, Liu. You should observe next time. You just might learn something." Cantowicz smirked, pulled a pair of tortoise shell framed sunglasses from his breast pocket. He exhaled a hot breath on the glass, and began to polish the deep amber lenses with a crisp linen handkerchief.

"But the connective tissue on the Chimera is tough as nails. How did you connect the J-Pouch without a long hard fight?"

"The stoma was a battle, true, but the J-Pouch was a breeze, because there isn't one."

"What?" asked Liu. "Did you end up with a K-Pouch or some other configuration based on your findings once the Chimera was open? Seems to me that would have taken even longer."

"No special configuration was necessary. The J-Pouch was never done, because Mr. Sutherland *and I* decided against it."

"You and Mr. Sutherland?" Liu sprang from his seat on the floor as if hot coals burned beneath him. "These are *my* patients. You dare breach *my* chain of command?"

"A J-Pouch? It was a dumb idea, and you know it. I simply pointed out to Mr. Sutherland that spending the time and resources on the Chimera wasn't cost effective. What can I say? I can't help it that he agreed with me."

"Why you back stabbing butcher!" Liu pushed past Dr. Cantowicz to look in on Zhū. "You're fired! Take your minions with you, Cantowicz! You're through!"

Dr. Cantowicz artfully placed his spectacles in their customary resting place on top of his head, in his dark, wavy hair. "Pfft. We'll see about that." He tossed the keys to his imported sports car into the air, and walked away chuckling to himself.

Liu dragged himself, a nearly lifeless corpse down the hallway to the surgical suite, and the recovery room where the Chimera lay, in the Neverland of anesthesia.

With the sheet pulled back, he was able to examine the Chimera's newly installed stoma with attached ostomy bag. The red portal that was the new exit for the Chimera's bodily waste was already showing signs of healing. Despite what he thought of the devious Dr. Cantowicz, the sutures were an expertly crafted thing of beauty. "The bastard does fine work," grumbled Liu under his breath.

Nurse Vicki burst in, interrupting Dr. Liu's examination. "It's Abby! Come quick!"

Chapter 32

Too Many Chiefs

"Give it to me straight, Liu. I want every detail of Abby's post-operative condition." Maxwell Sutherland filled a pipe with his signature chocolate cherry tobacco blend.

"The complications are many. Infection, anastomotic stricture, intra-abdominal abscess, and peritonitis, just to name a few."

"In layman's terms?" Maxwell puffed.

Dr. Liu took a deep breath. "It means that although the surgery was a success, Abby is still a very sick little girl."

"I thought that the colon transplant would help her, but it seems that you have just made matters worse!"

"Rest assured we are doing our best__"

"Best? I'm not quite so sure, that you, Dr. are doing your best! Why I ought to have Dr. Cantowicz take over from here!"

"Speaking of Cantowicz, he just informed me that the two of you made a decision regarding the Chimera without consulting me."

"Yes. What of it? Cantowicz explained your plans to create a replacement rectum using the Chimera's own small intestine. He and I decided that such a procedure was an unnecessary expenditure of manpower, and money."

An enraged Liu clenched his fists at his sides, as he tried to keep his composure. "An unnecessary expenditure? I'd say it is much more than that!" Liu's voice rose a squeaky octave. "It is our moral obligation to give that beast some dignity in his destruction!"

"Here we go again." Maxwell exhaled his displeasure in choppy puffs.

"It is our moral obligation, yours and mine. I agree that because Abby is human, that her needs come first, but to leave the Chimera with a bag for the rest of its life is unconscionable."

“Save the hyperbole, Liu. I know that human patients live active healthy lives with the stoma, and the bag. If it’s good enough for them__”

“Those are situations where there may be no other medical or financial option. Neither were a problem in the case of the Chimera. We had the ability to restore him as closely to normal as possible, and the funds to do it.”

Maxwell choked on the barbs of Liu’s indictment. “Don’t you dare tell me how to spend my own damned money? If I decide it is superfluous, that is the end of it. Before you resort to that old ‘quality of life’ sermon you are so fond of pontificating, get out of my office.”

Chapter 33

Tomorrow Never Comes

In the weeks and months to follow, Abby's condition gradually improved to the point where Dr. Cantowicz and his team went on to other projects far away from the Sutherland Mansion. Maxwell had also resumed his habit of extensive business travel. All of this came as a welcomed relief to Liu and his associates.

In his guilt stricken heart and mind, Liu opted to continue with enhancing the Chimera's life by introducing as much media to him as possible, be it children's books or games and videos. If he was responsible for destroying the Chimera physically, he would also be the one to develop him mentally. Not much of a tradeoff, perhaps, but it did wonders for Liu's own mental health, thinking that in some small way, he was giving something back to the creature.

Four walls, a warm bed and a stack of books was not enough to suppress Zhū's growing sense of isolation. Nurse Vicki and Dr. Liu made their daily rounds, monitoring his health, and wellbeing. Physical and occupational therapists also worked daily on maintaining his motor and cognitive skills. Since being moved to the groundskeeper's cottage on the Southwestern corner of the Sutherland Estate's grounds, his vitals and his body was always strong, but Zhū's heart ached.

"See Abby?" asked Zhū.

"Maybe tomorrow," Vicki replied.

Maxwell Sutherland had taken to a special affinity for security cameras. Lots of them. In fact, it was nearly impossible to do anything on the Estate without being watched. She reached up, to move the lens pointed at her face as she updated the Chimera's charts. Vicki jumped back as an alarm sounded.

"Please do not handle the security equipment!" A shrill voice of ill-tempered tin chided her. Startled, she jumped nearly out of her skin. The camera spun, and the lens adjusted to zoom in on her.

The Chimera looked up with little interest before diverting his attention back to his newest tome.

Vicki thought of the overabundance of watchful eyes and shuddered. “The constant surveillance gives me the creeps! I suppose you’re listening to every word I utter too?” She put her face just inches from the camera in accusation, but the ever observant monitor behind the machine offered no reply. “Yep.” Vicki organized her files and made for the door. “I thought so.”

Zhū turned a page, and looked at the back of Vicki as she fled for the slightest bit of privacy. “Snort. Maybe tomorrow.”

Chapter 34

No Bones About It

Staff members raced to attend to the luggage and person of their employer. It had been another long business trip. Maxwell shed his coat and hat as he could bear their weight no longer. His upright posture withered and sagged when Dr. Liu entered.

"I got here as quickly as I could," said Maxwell with a quiver in his voice. "How bad is she?"

Dr. Liu held a metal clad medical chart in his right hand, tapping it into the palm of his left hand in search of a rhythm for the sad song of Abby's latest setback.

"The disease is on the move once again."

"Don't you mean still?" asked Maxwell.

"Since the J-Pouch surgery, Abby did have a couple of years to recover. We hoped that once and for all, we had beaten this thing, this hyper-evolved cancer, whatever it is. Unfortunately for Abby, it is back, and more aggressive than ever."

"I thought she had a simple stress fracture, from her school dance?"

"That's what we told you to get you here. There's no sense in worrying you to the point that your own safety would be compromised."

"I'll decide how much worry I can handle. Give it to me straight."

"Walk with me to the lab, I want to show you something."

The burnished marble entry gave way to acres of oriental carpets, ending at the security door of the sterile surgical wing. Antimicrobial tiles squeaked under their shoes. Dr. Liu flipped on a light panel where x-rays were displayed.

"This is the stress fracture we told you about." Liu scrolled through his computer screen. "And this, is the source of the break."

"Her bone marrow?"

"Yes, the mass in red is where the disease is now lodged."

"Okay, so you'll perform a bone marrow transplant using that thing, the Chimera. I'm sure its marrow is healthy. You have my permission to proceed."

"I have directed the team to prep the Chimera."

"As for Abby?"

"When this latest development was discovered, I took the liberty of starting her on chemo and radiation. Now that you have officially signed off, we will get her into pre-op immediately. Dr. Cantowicz and team B will act as the harvest team, just as in past procedures." Liu reached to the intercom. "Nurse, please send Cantowicz in."

"You rang?" asked Cantowicz as he adjusted the draw string on his scrubs.

"I want no infighting. Promise me the rivalry between you will be set aside until my daughter is out of the woods. Do I make myself clear?"

"Perfectly," said Cantowicz. Dr. Liu nodded.

Cantowicz made for the door. "If you'll excuse me, I have a patient to attend to."

Chapter 35

Eight Hours of Power

The bright lamp that hung over Abby shone with the intensity of ten suns. As she was being transferred from the gurney to the table, Dr. Liu spotted something unusual on her thigh. He pulled back a corner of her gown to get a better look.

"What the heck?"

"That's new. A lump?" asked Nurse Vicki.

"Scaple, and clamps. I have to get a better look at this! Oh my God! It has spread! How can this be? It's everywhere! Quick! Get Cantowicz!"

As usual, Cantowicz had finished the harvest quickly, and was on his way to the showers when Vicki burst in.

"Dr. Liu needs you, immediately!"

"Where's the fire, Liu?" asked an irritated Cantowicz.

"Here. Have a look for yourself."

"Well, that is something. All of this even after chemo *and* radiation? How?"

"I have never seen something so resistant and aggressive. Looks like your easy harvest just turned into a very long day."

Cantowicz stood with his hands on his hips. "Yeah, maybe someday you'll learn to just do it my way to start with." He was smug, happy to be in control of the situation. "Pfft. Give me about eight hours. I'll take what you need."

Chapter 36

Miss Thing

Nurse Vicki pulled the blankets from her unwilling patient. "Up and at 'em, young lady! Physical therapy will be here any minute."

"It hurts too much." Abby whined. "I just had major surgery you know!"

"Yes, I was there, now stop your bellyaching, and get up. Here, just put a little weight on me."

"I can't"

"You can, and you will!"

The therapist tapped on the door. And wheeled a chair to Abby's bedside.

"You can do this," said the muscular man.

"But__"

"Yes, I know it is very soon after your surgery, but it is crucial that we get you up and moving ASAP. Ready? On three."

Vicki and the therapist lifted a defiant and screaming Abby from the bed to her wheelchair.

"Wow!" exclaimed Vicki.

"I can't help it! I told you I was in pain!" Abby continued her tirade.

"No." Vicki let out a sigh. "It's not your bad attitude, Miss Thing. I just don't remember when you got to be as tall as me. She patted the side of the wheelchair. "Now off with you! And don't give the therapist a hard time. He's just trying to help you."

Chapter 37

The Conspiracy

Four weeks had passed, but Abby made little effort in re-learning how to walk. The therapist was at his wits end.

"I don't know what else to do with her. I have never had a patient fight so hard *not* to improve."

Vicki dispensed the pain pills for Abby's evening dose. "You're too hard on yourself. She's a good kid, just has lived most of her life fighting this horrible thing, so now she's fighting you. Don't worry. I've cared for her since she was a little girl. I know her well. She'll come around."

"I'm not so sure she will, and if she doesn't show improvement, Mr. Sutherland has threatened my dismissal." The therapist soothed his own temples with brawny hands. "I need this job. I still have student loans to pay."

Vicki shot the therapist a sly look, remembering the abundance of cameras and listening devices, she began to scribble a note on a pharmaceutical company note pad, then handed it to the therapist motioning with a finger over her lips that he should not read it out loud.

I know exactly who can inspire Abby. If you want to save your job, I'll need a little help. Deal?

He nodded in agreement. "Deal."

Chapter 38

Stand and Deliver

When it came time for PT the next morning Abby was already defiant and grumbling.

"I don't want to go. It hurts too much. Besides, I am making no improvement. It's a huge waste of time,"

"I know for a fact that you want to go, because it will be your best session ever." Vicki unfolded a robe for Abby to wear with her back to the camera. Inside the garment, the label had a single word written in laundry marker.

ZHŪ.

"Really?" asked Abby. "Pinky swear?"

"Ha, ha! Yep. It will be your best session, as long as you remain positive, and work hard. Pinky swear." She winked at Abby, and smiled. How she missed seeing Abby in a good mood.

Vicki wheeled Abby down a series of long corridors, stopping just outside the gymnasium.

"Aren't we going in?" asked an impatient Abby.

Vicki eyed the security camera, and checked the time. "In a minute."

The camera's red light clicked off. "Perfect timing!" declared Vicki, satisfied that she had accurately timed the security office's coffee break. The double doors opened with a mechanical grind.

Vicki wheeled an eager Abby to a gurney past the treadmills, weights, and machinery.

"Zhū Zhū!" She cried. Tears welled in the corners of her eyes. "Quick! Help me up!"

Abby's muscles had atrophied to the point where standing was impossible without nearly teetering over. The Therapist and Vicki steadied her at Zhū's bedside.

"We'll leave the two of you alone." Vicki checked the time again. "You have ten minutes."

Abby sat up, studying Zhū as she tried to get comfortable on the edge of the bed. He looked different than she remembered. She was aware of how much she had changed as well, practically all grown up, but Zhū looked like an old man playing dress up in a tattered pig suit. His hair, once stubbly and dark was now splotchy patches of tarnished silver. His incisors had grown into a long set of yellowed tusks, and his eyes, once inquisitive and bright were clouded companions to a furrowed set of crow's feet. It startled Abby, but she tried her best not to let it show.

"I'm so sorry I haven't been allowed to see you. It's this disease, in my bone marrow now and my muscles." Her voice dropped to a whisper. "It's eating me alive."

"Snort. Snort."

"It got into my leg." Abby pushed herself up at an angle, still unable to find a comfortable position to sit, pressing the mattress at Zhū's side as he did. Suddenly she looked down at her own hand with a question in her eyes. She felt along the top sheet, tracing the edge of Zhū's legs to discover that he had only one.

"Your leg! My God! What have they done?" She threw her arms around him. Her tears soaked into his hospital gown. "This is so unfair! How dare they do this to you?" She gripped him tight as she wailed at the injustice of it all. Zhū lay silent and detached from her grief. He did not return her embrace. "To put you through this," she continued, "and for what? I can barely stand." She sobbed. "I am stuck in that stupid wheelchair."

"Squeaal! Squeaaaaal!" Zhū pushed her away. A bewildered Abby wiped her eyes on the sleeve of her fluffy cotton robe. "Squeaaaaal! Squeaaaal!" He became more enraged.

"I don't understand."

Zhū took hold of Abby's crutch and used it to push her wheel chair clear to the other side of the gymnasium. "Squeal Squeal!"

"Hey! What are you doing? I need that!"

"Snort. Abby walk."

"But I can't, I told you!"

Hot breath, and drips of sweat formed on the fleshy flat end of Zhū's nose. His breathing was erratic. His snorts and squeals echoed through the room. Abby saw a fire had replaced the murky hollow in Zhū's eyes, and the very first time, she was afraid of him. He threw the crutch so hard it landed with a clatter at the doors across the room.

"ABBY WALK!" Zhū ground his teeth snarling, and bearing them at her. He shoved her a second time, with a force that upended her off of the bed. She grabbed at the sheets to pull herself to stand. His agitation escalated, and so did Abby's fear. His snorts turned to a series of guttural barking and baying. "WALK!"

Abby gasped at the horror her friend had become. Terror told her legs to run, and run fast! She fled as quickly as possible, swerving and unsteady on a borrowed limb that failed to carry her. The double doors flew open. The therapist stood wide eyed, struggling to understand just how his most reluctant patient just ran to him, and collapsed into his arms.

Chapter 39

A Change of Heart

In the conference room adjoining Maxwell's office, Nurse Vicki, and Dr. Liu sat, together, but alone in their own minds. Occasionally, they would share a fleeting glance, but neither dared start a conversation. Neither could speak of their current dilemma, for in speaking of it, both new that it would leave the realm of thought, and become reality, a truth that neither of them wished to face.

The double doors swung wide open, partially obscuring the Hudson River landscape mural on the wall. "I'm expected to speak at The G-8 in Tokyo." Maxwell checked his watch, and huffed while impatiently counting time zones and calculating lost travel time. "What is it now? It had better be good."

Dr. Liu remained seated. "Another development in Abby's condition. No, it is not good. Perhaps you should sit down?"

"I'm fine." Maxwell put his outstretched hands, palms down on the long table. He leaned over to stare down at them, a not so subtle reminder that it was he who was in charge. "As I said, I have a summit to attend. I do not have all day."

"It is Abby's heart." Dr. Liu lowered the lights with a few clicks, and opened his files to a display screen on the opposite side of the room. "This mass to the left ventricle? A tumor beneath the pericardium. Our scans show that it has already started to spread into the heart muscle."

Maxwell's eyes closed with the drop of his head. He abandoned his stance of intimidation to run his hands through his hair. He paced while keeping his eyes glued to the images Dr. Liu provided. In a few minutes, he composed himself, and sat, head up, shoulders thrown back, a man resigned to action. "So when can you do it?"

"Do it?" Liu pushed his glasses to his eyes. His brow furrowed.

"Yes, the heart transplant. When can you have both teams ready? I'm sure you have already alerted Cantowicz to this latest development. What's the timeline? Maybe I can deliver my speech via internet link?"

Vicki put her elbows on the table, resting her head between her hands, fingers laced over her ears. Still, she heard every word.

"Mr. Sutherland, I'm afraid you don't grasp the whole of the situation, or the gravity of these developments. If we proceed with the heart transplant, the Chimera *will die*."

Maxwell began counting on his fingers, he closed one eye to aid concentration as he did the math. "The way I see it, in ten years, fifteen surgeries, four organ donations," Maxwell scratched his chin, "not to mention the skin, bone, marrow and muscle harvests, I'd say the Chimera has more than paid for itself. Expensive, sure, but Abby is still alive. I'd say that was money well spent."

Vicki shook her head in her hands, rolling her eyes while she mused. "He just doesn't get it."

Maxwell tilted his head. "What is there to get, Liu? Nurse? I'm sure that you can make provisions to extract any viable tissue for future use. Cryogenically preserve anything Abby can make use of. As for the rest of it, if my brokers are shrewd, which by the way, they are, I can turn a tidy profit on the black market. Win, win, I'd say."

"I can't believe my ears!" Vicki's forearms fell over her head that now rested flat on the conference table top.

"What has gotten into the two of you?" Asked Maxwell.

Dr. Liu stood, putting his hands on his hips. "We are saddened by the possible loss of the Chimera. Especially given the likelihood that Abby's disease will likely migrate to other areas."

"So?" asked Maxwell. "I'll just buy another one. Problem solved!"

Vicki peeked out from her forearm fortress, as it offered no protection anyway. "Just buy another one? Create a life for the sole purpose of destroying it, and when it has outlived its usefulness, make another thing to kill?"

Non-plussed, Maxwell pressed a button in the center of the table's console. Two armed security guards appeared. "Escort the nurse to the lockers.

See that she has gathered all of her belongings, and escort her off of the property. I regret that after ten years of service, my daughter's wellbeing is no longer her priority."

"This is sick!" Vicki screamed. "You will rot in hell for this!" Her arms and legs flailed as the guards muscled her out of the room.

Dr. Liu slipped back into his chair, paralyzed while his mind considered all scenarios, relishing those that might, by some slim chance, save the Chimera from final destruction.

"Have you anything to add to the Nurse's objections?" Maxwell glared at Liu.

"Nurse Vicki and I have known the Chimera for the past decade. Just as with your daughter, Abby, we have grown somewhat attached. You specified that we should care for Abby as if she was our child. Over the years, we have developed the same attachment to the Chimera."

Maxwell checked his watch again. *Maybe I can still speak at the conference, and make it back in time to see Abby in post-op?*

"The Nurse was correct about one thing. Attachment to that thing? No! I do not get it. As for you, Liu, has your attachment, as you call it, for an abomination, a freak, a beast, has that irrational sympathy overshadowed your ability to honor your oath to take the very best care of my daughter? Are you so clouded and compromised that you won't save my daughter's life?"

"But the Chimera isn't an inanimate medical device as you would like to let yourself believe. It is a living, breathing life. It is capable of speech, rational thought, and love."

"Love?"

"He, I mean, *it*, loves Abby. I can see it in his eyes! And he is strong. I know that he could have escaped by overpowering the staff at any time, but he didn't! He stayed, allowing us to carve him up because he knew how sick she is. He stayed to save Abby."

"Need I remind you that purchasing the Chimera was *your* idea? Dr. Duan, the Chimera's creator was *your* contact?"

Dr. Liu hung his head. "Yes. I'll admit that I was ambitious, and fascinated by the prospect of what such an advanced medical technology might do for my career, and for Abby, but I never considered that the Chimera could be so__"

"Human?"

Liu let out with a lingering sigh.

"Yes."

Chapter 40

Daddy Dearest

"Daddy, this makes no sense. Dr. Liu always explained my illness to me as a sort of cancer, but one so advanced and rare that they have never seen it before." Abby crossed her arms in front of her.

"Yes. That is how he has also explained it to me. What part is confusing you?" Maxwell reached for Abby's hand that remained locked at her chest.

"Well, I've done my homework, and there really isn't any such thing as heart cancer. Maybe they just have it wrong this time."

"Baby," Maxwell laid a hand on Abby's shoulder. "I wish that they are wrong about this just as much as you do, but I've seen the images. The cells. They are the same, and they are back."

Abby took two steps away from her father. His hand fell from her shoulder to his side. He reached for her as she took yet another step, increasing the distance between them. "I'm almost eighteen. I'm not your baby anymore!"

Maxwell's chin dropped to his chest. He let out a small chuckle.

"I don't see any humor in this."

"I'm sorry. It just occurred to me that you have been telling me that you aren't a baby from the very first time you learned to speak." He took a deep breath in order to compose himself as he frequently did when negotiating his business deals. "You are an intelligent, capable young woman, Abby. I'm very proud of how you've grown."

"That's right! I am grown, and capable of making my own decisions. I'm not having any more surgeries. You can't make me!"

In truth, Maxwell Sutherland's immense wealth and power made it remarkably easy to force the hand of others. His rivals and allies alike did exactly what he wanted them to do. None dared cross him. No one except the frail teen with dishwater blonde hair and hazel eyes ever threatened to topple his rule. He could force her to undergo the heart transplant, and risk that Abby would likely hate him for it.

But Maxwell Sutherland was risk tolerant. Making perilous choices in business made him rich. Peril was part of his DNA. Abby's ire was a gamble he was willing to take to keep her alive. He played his hand, leading with a bluff.

"But you will surely die, Abby. I can't imagine this world without you,"

She traced the carved mahogany panel with her fingertip. "I can't imagine it either, but Daddy, I can't do this anymore! This isn't life. It is only little doses of isolation and pain. I'm begging you! Please, Daddy, you have to let me go." Her knees shook. The gravity of her declaration made her dizzy and weak. Abby grasped the molding to avoid fainting to the floor. Her father rushed to her, scooping her up, then landing her in the comfort and protection of a massive wingchair. He knelt in front of her as she sobbed.

"Very well." Maxwell glanced at an old silver framed photo on his desk. A picture of him and his wife on their wedding day. He took another deep breath while wiping his daughter's tears with his thumb. "Although I vehemently disagree with your decision, and as much as it pains me to say so, you are right. You are a grown woman, and it is *your* life, *your* decision to make. I won't force you to do anything you don't want to do." He brushed her cheek with the back of his hand.

Abby looked at him through the filmy blur of her sorrow, at the man she knew to be her father, but lately had not recognized as such. He was different than the man she knew as a child. In his generosity, he had become a miser of time. His love for her given as a check that he might write to a charity, as a consequence, and obligation of his station. His love felt like something he gave to gain favor from his peers, or a tax break from the government. His affection had come to have conditions attached. Conditions, that she must always be brave, smile, and most importantly, obey. The watery distortion of tears gave her an odd clarity, a reckoning that told her disease ridden heart of hearts not to trust him, but this was *her father*. How could she not?

Her eyes narrowed and focused on him. She stayed silent for a moment. Her breath shallow, and labored. Her heart hurt both from the emotional strain, and physical deterioration of her condition. Maxwell Sutherland knelt at her side, but the weight of his words felt as if he were standing on her chest. She threw her arms around him, holding on tight, clinging to her father, and to a world that she had neither the strength to endure, nor the power to leave.

"You will respect my wishes?" asked Abby with a strained voice.

"I will respect your wishes. I promise."

Chapter 41

The Unconscious Conscience

"I hate this thing!" snarled Liu under his breath, as he removed his phone from the pocket of his lab coat.

The incessant buzzing, ringing, and chimes had worn on his nerves to the point where he was ready to chuck the thing at the wall. He had no time or interest in distractions. He had to think.

Buzz. Buzz. Ding!

Another message from Vicki. The dozens of voice mail messages, and texts all had the same content. Even though she was fired, and physically removed from the Sutherland Estate, nothing would keep her from doing what she considered her moral obligation.

"Please don't do this! Killing the Chimera is wrong, and you know it!"

She was right, and Liu did know it, but for him, it was not so simple, his obligation was to protect the Chimera. It was also his duty to save Abby Sutherland, especially given the fact that he had the means to do so. How to reconcile the two?

Buzz. Buzz. Ding!

Vicki sent an old photo of Zhū and Abby playing together when they were both small. It was evident by the look in their eyes that they were devoted to each other, and shared a special bond. Liu studied the picture. He paced while deciding what to do.

Emotional blackmail. Great. Thanks, Vicki.

"I respect your opinion, but will handle this in my own way." Liu responded then blocked Vicki's number. He went back to pacing alongside a wall of windows. As he weighed his actions as well as opportunity, Liu failed to notice Abby driving a golf cart to the edge of the Sutherland Estate, to the cottage that had become Zhū's home.

Tap, tap, tap.

No answer. *Where is everybody? Vicki? The physical therapist?* Abby wondered. She leaned on her cane as she let herself in.

"Zhū-Zhū? Are you here? It's me. Abby."

To her right was a pile of medical charts, books and half eaten bags of snacks on a long white counter. She spied the odd array of science, literature, and junk food. A blinking red camera light followed her as she continued her search. Around the corner, she found him, asleep in a window seat, propped up on a mound of pillows, a book open on his lap, eyeglasses askew, tilted sideways on his face. He seemed so peaceful, and so frail, she hesitated to disturb him, but she had to speak with him, one last time before her heart failed, and she was gone forever.

"Zhū-Zhū." Her voice as low as a whisper. "I don't mean to disturb you, but__"

"Abby? Snort. Snort." His spectacles fell from their precarious position into the open book. Zhū blinked his nap away, and his diminished eyesight into focus. Fuzzy as she was, Zhū would recognize her anywhere.

"I came to apologize. I'm sorry about how we left things, you know, the last time we saw each other, in the gym?"

"Snort. Snort. Snort."

"I am really sorry, Zhū Zhū. Please? Forgive me?" She shook, nervous that he may again growl and bear his teeth at her. Her cane kept her steady, and upright.

Zhū's shoulders slumped as he bowed his head. "Snort. Snort."

A lump swelled in the back of Abby's throat. "No, Zhū-Zhū. You aren't to blame. I understand. At least," her voice cracked. "I__I think I understand why you became so angry with me."

"Snort Snort. Squeal!"

"Please, let me stay. I understand that when they took your leg, they took a piece of your self-worth, as well as your mobility. In giving up, I had something of yours that was stolen from you, and I failed to appreciate what you lost. But look! I'm trying hard, and doing very well!"

Zhū put his book aside, and fumbled to put the glasses back on his face and smiled. "Abby walk."

"I can get around with a little help from the cane, and in no time, I'd probably be running, but__"

Zhū tilted his head in question.

She moved toward him, keeping as strong and straight a posture as she could manage while crossing the room. "May I sit with you?"

Zhū looked up at her over the top of his glasses and smiled, showing his tiny teeth as she always remembered him. He patted the cushion at his side.

"Zhū-Zhū, I didn't come only to apologize. I came to__" Her face flushed red, and flooded with tears. "I came to thank you. You have endured so much for me, but I have to say goodbye." She gasped for air, hyperventilating in her grief. "While I still have time."

His round eyes never blinked, for fear of missing an instant of time with her.

"It's my heart. It is sick, just like my kidneys, colon and my leg." Whaa! Sniff. Sniff. She blew her nose, and tried to remain calm but the tears would not stop. Hearing her own words, spoken out loud, about her diseased heart made her abbreviated life a cruel reality.

Zhū sat up straight, his eyes darted around, searching the room.

"No. Don't worry. They won't hurt you anymore. This horror is going to be over soon."

Zhū took Abby's hand, placing it on his heart with a calm that disturbed her.

"No! You don't understand, Zhū-Zhū. You'll die! And for what? A few months, or a couple of years if I'm lucky? In no time, this plague will move on to another place in my body, and I'll be facing more surgery. No! I have heard my father talking to Dr. Liu. He's thinking about getting another chimera to replace you. It is a never-ending nightmare! This has to stop! It's sick!"

"But Abby will die?"

Sniff. "Yes, but I have come to terms with it, at least I'm trying to. It's okay. My father and I have discussed it. I have asked him to let me go."

Zhū's gray bristles of hair stood on end at the mention of Maxwell Sutherland, and the pain he inflicted on both he and Abby.

"He knows. I just can't go through this anymore." Abby snuggled into Zhū's shoulder, as he slowly stroked her hair.

He placed her hand back on his chest.

"Oh, Zhū-Zhū, now you see, don't you? It is wrong, what's been happening! I don't know, maybe my father's intentions were good at the beginning, but this has to stop!"

The two friends sat in silence as the daylight faded. Each trying to understand the incomprehensible reality of their lives. Abby snuggled back into his shoulder as she wept.

"I don't want your heart Zhū-Zhū. I want to live, I do__ but not like this." The tears flowed, this time, for both of them.

"Abby already has Zhū-Zhū's heart."

"Stop it! Please! I don't want you to die, Zhū-Zhū." Sob. "I want you to live."

He shook his head, no. "Snort Snort." Her hand caressed to his sagging cheek. His eyes involuntarily closed at the warmth of her touch. "Not like this."

Chapter 42

Promises Kept

A bright white light forced Abby's lids to squint a layer of protection from the glare. She was far too tired to wake up, but the efforts to turn her head away from the blaze didn't work. In struggling to roll her whole body over, she found that she was being held flat on her back.

Someone turn out that light. I need to sleep. But she could form no sound to match the words in her head. Her eyes opened to the blaze of a surgical lamp above her. She knew the light well. It hung in midair as a sentry, guarding a valuable prisoner. It suddenly occurred to Abby that she was captive, indeed. Try as she might to scream for help, she found that the tube down her throat, and mask on her face would not allow her to make much more than a whimper.

But, wait! Why am I in surgery? Abby asked herself, and anyone nearby who might notice her plight. *Can someone tell me what is happening?* The pressure in her chest grew to a sharp pain, so excruciating that tears were the only method her body had to mitigate her agony. There and then__ she knew. She was keenly aware of the stitches in her chest, and a heartbeat that seemed both stronger and quicker than her own. It was true. Her Father had betrayed her.

How could you? You promised me!

Abby struggled to see what she could through the glass separating her O.R. from a corridor, a lab, and the lockers. The fixture above her framed the view in the manner of a waking dream, too real to be true. In the hall, she could see a gurney against the wall. The white sheet covered most of the corpse, but a grayed pink cloven hand hung battered and lifeless over the bed's edge.

"Zhū-Zhū!" Abby screamed into the tubes and wires. *"Noooooo!"*

Dr. Liu walked toward the gurney while pulling down his mask. He threw his head back for a moment, seeming to compose himself. He tucked the arm under the sheet as a pair of orderlies joined him, to push the body of Zhū away.

Abby continued to scream for someone, anyone, to wake her from her nightmare, but no one heard her over the skirmish of Dr. Liu being dragged away by two towering armed guards. The gurney with the body of her dead friend was wheeled out of sight.

Voices gathered at the other end of the corridor. Her chest throbbed, the devices to which she was connected blinked, and buzzed in alarm, sounding for a patient no one expected would be awake so soon. But the hall was too busy for anyone to take notice. Still, Abby screamed, in mourning for Zhū, the love for her father now lost, and the peaceful death she would never be allowed to have.

She recognized the voices of her father, and Dr. Cantowicz. She watched them trade congratulatory handshakes, and a large briefcase with a slim man she did not recognize, but his starched lab coat suggested that he was another doctor. The strange man smiled, and bowed deeply upon receiving the briefcase. He then motioned for something. A second gurney wheeled up to the men. The form bound to it, unmistakable.

Abby thrashed, and yelled, tugging at the binding in terror to free herself. She tried to blink the image away, but could not deny what she was seeing. Her cries still muffled whimpers.

"Another___? Noooo!"

CPSIA information can be obtained
at www.ICGtesting.com
Printed in the USA
BVHW080009280619
552175BV00001B/39/P

9 781545 664261